MW01236029

THE GUNSMITH

#402 KIDNAP A GUNSMITH

PRO SE ⚖ PRESS

THE GUNSMITH #402: KIDNAP A GUNSMITH
A Pro Se Press Publication

All rights reserved under U.S. and International copyright law. This book is licensed only for the private use of the purchaser. May not be copied, scanned, digitally reproduced, or printed for re-sale, may not be uploaded on shareware or free sites, or used in any other manner without the express written permission of the author and/or publisher. Thank you for respecting the hard work of the author.

Kidnap A Gunsmith is a work of historical fiction. Many of the important historical events, figures, and locations are as accurately portrayed as possible. In keeping with a work of fiction, various events and occurrences were invented by the author.

Edited by Tommy Hancock
Editor in Chief, Pro Se Productions—Tommy Hancock
Submissions Editor—Rachel Lampi
Director of Corporate Operations—Kristi King-Morgan
Publisher & Pro Se Productions, LLC-Chief Executive Officer—Fuller Bumpers

Cover Art by Jeffrey Hayes
Print Production and Book Design by Percival Constantine
New Pulp Logo Design by Sean E. Ali
New Pulp Seal Design by Cari Reese

Pro Se Productions, LLC
133 1/2 Broad Street
Batesville, AR, 72501
870-834-4022

editorinchief@prose-press.com
www.prose-press.com

THE GUNSMITH #402: KIDNAP A GUNSMITH © 2015 Robert J. Randisi

Published in digital form by Piccadilly Publishing, June 2015

THE GUNSMITH

#402 KIDNAP A GUNSMITH

J.R. ROBERTS

PRO SE PRESS

ONE

Clint Adams rode into Casa Grande, Arizona in one hell of a bad mood.

First, as soon as he entered Arizona and dismounted to camp the first night the heel of his right boot snapped off. He had stopped in two other towns since, but none of them had a cobbler who could fix the boot, and he resisted buying a completely new pair.

By the time he was a day from Casa Grande he had run out of coffee and beans, and the next morning Eclipse, his Darley Arabian, had thrown a shoe.

So he didn't actually ride into town, but walked, leading Eclipse behind him. He knew he could have ridden the horse with only three shoes, but he didn't want to take a chance on injuring that bare hoof.

So they both limped into Casa Grande.

One of the first people he ran into was a boy about twelve years old.

"Excuse me, son," he said, stopping the boy as he crossed the street.

"Wow, Mister, that's some horse."

"Yes, he is."

"What's wrong with him?"

"Nothing serious," Clint said. "He just threw a shoe."

"We got us a real good blacksmith and hostler over to the livery," the boy said, pointing.

"That's good to hear," Clint said, "and I sort of threw a shoe myself." He showed the boy his broken heel. "Is there a cobbler in town?"

"Yes, sir," the boy said. "You'll pass him on the way to the livery, on the left side of the street."

"Thank you, son." Clint tossed the kid two bits.

"Wow. Thanks," the boy said, catching it deftly with one hand. "My name's Nathan Tanner. You need anythin' else in town you just look fer me."

"I'll do that, Nathan," Clint said. "Thanks."

The boy ran off to complete whatever errand he had been on when Clint stopped him. Clint continued walking down Main Street, drawing looks from the town folk coming out to start their mornings.

After walking several more streets he saw the cobbler the boy had been talking about. There was no name over the door or on the window, but there were leather products like holsters and boots in the window.

He approached, looped Eclipse's reins loosely over a hitching post, and went inside. He was immediately struck by the smell of leather, which was pleasant.

A man came out of a back room at that moment, middle aged with a big belly and red-but-pleasant face.

"Can I help ya?"

"I hope so," Clint said. He held up the heel that had come off his boot. "I threw a heel."

"Bring it over to the counter."

They both walked to the counter, the man easing his bulk behind it.

"Give it here," he said.

Clint handed him the heel.

"Oh yeah," he said, "I can fix this."

"Can you do it quickly?" Clint asked. "My horse also threw a shoe. I need to take him to your hostler."

"Won't take long," the man promised. "Let me have your boot."

Clint looked around, saw a wooden chair nearby, so he sat and yanked off his boot. The man came from around the counter and took it.

"I'll just take it into the shop in back and be right back," he said. "Should take a few nails, is all."

"Thanks."

"Look around," the man invited. "Maybe you need a new holster or somethin'."

"I'll take a look."

The man nodded, satisfied that his sales pitch had been accepted, and went into the back room through a curtained doorway.

Clint stood up and limped around on one boot and a sock to look at the man's wares. From what he could see of some of the hand-tooled holsters, the man knew his business. In the back of the room there was even a brand new saddle with beautiful work on it.

While he was looking the front door opened and a lady walked in. She was wearing a blue dress with a matching bonnet, her long blonde hair wore down around her shoulders. She had a firm body and smooth, pale skin, but was not a girl. As Clint watched her he judged her to be almost forty.

"Oh!" she said, startled when she saw him.

"I'm sorry,' he said. "I didn't mean to scare you."

"Not at all," she said. "I was just...I wasn't frightened. Is Mr. Bennett here?"

"If he's the fella with the red face and big belly, he's in the back fixing my boot heel."

"Well," she said, "I suppose that describes him very well."

"I can go back there and get him, if you like," he offered.

She looked down at his feet, one booted and one with just a sock, and said, "I wouldn't want you to walk around here and step on a nail or something."

"Well," he answered, "he did say he wouldn't be long."

They both fell silent for a moment and could hear the rat-a-tat-tat of a hammer from the back room.

"I'm just picking something up," she said. "I can, uh, wait."

"There's a chair, here," he said, moving it a little closer to her.

"Thank you." She sat, but when she realized she'd have to be looking up at him, she decided to stand again. "You're a stranger in town."

"Yes, I was rode in—well, I walked in."

"Is that your beautiful horse out front?"

"It is," he said. "He did the same thing I did, and threw a shoe."

"Ah...bad luck."

"I thought so," he said, "until now."

She blushed.

TWO

Her name was Gloria Knight. She lived in town, had a store of her own—a boutique, she called it—and, by asking the right questions and listening attentively he surmised that she was not married.

"Clint Adams?" she said, when he told her his name. "That name is..."

At that point Mr. Bennett came out of the back room, carrying Clint's boot.

"Oh, Miss Knight," he said, "I'm sorry to keep you waiting."

"That's all right, George," she said. "I was having a nice conversation with Mr. Adams. You may finish your business with him."

"Here ya go, Mr....Adams?" Bennett's eye popped just a bit as he handed Clint his boot.

"Thanks," Clint said. "What do I owe you?"

"Uh, oh, not much," Bennett said, nervously. "Uh, in fact, I don't think I should ever charge you, uh—"

Clint handed him some coins and said, "There, that should cover it."

"Um, oh yeah, yeah, that covers it just fine, Mr. Adams," Bennett said.

Clint turned to Gloria Knight and said, "It was a pleasure to meet you, Miss Knight."

"The same here, Mr. Adams."

Clint turned and went to the door. As he went out he heard Bennett ask Gloria, "Do you know who that was?"

*****

Clint walked Eclipse to the livery stable on his repaired heel and entered. From outside he had heard the sound of a hammer on an anvil, as now he saw the big man with the leather apron standing at the anvil and forge. When he looked up, Clint could see the man was in his 50's, with a grey fringe of hair around a bald pate.

"Help ya? Say, that's a mighty fine lookin' animal." He put down the hammer and tongs he was holding, wiped his hands on a rag, and stepped forward. "That a Darley Arabian?"

"It is."

"Mighty fine lookin', yes sir," the man said.

"He tossed a shoe just outside of town," Clint said. "I walked him in."

"Good hinking'," the man said, lifting Eclipse's left foreleg to have a look. "Wouldn't wanna damage an animal like this."

Clint was surprised that Eclipse stood quietly and allowed the man to touch him. He figured the man must have had a good touch.

"I can fix this easy," the man said, straightening up. "Passin' through?"

"I thought I'd stay a day or two."

"Well, if you wanna put him up here I'll take good care of him. And I won't charge you much. Be a pleasure to have him in my barn."

"You take care of him and charge me your regular fees," Clint said. "I'll just take my rifle and saddlebags."

Eclipse stood calmly, and after Clint had removed his belongings the hostler took the animal's reins to lead him away.

"You must be good," Clint said. "He don't take to people."

"Me and horses," the man said, "we understand each other. I'll unsaddle him, rub him down, and feed 'im, and then take care of that shoe."

"What's your name?" Clint asked.

"Folks just call me Hoss."

Clint shook hands with the man and said, "Clint. How many hotels you got in town?"

"We got three," Hoss said, "and they're all pretty good. One's pretty cheap, but you really can't go wrong."

"Thanks," Clint said. "I'll just stop at the first one I come to."

"Check back with me later, you'll see I done right by this big guy."

"I'm sure you will."

*****

Clint left the livery stable and within two blocks came to a hotel called The Shrewsbury. He entered and approached the front desk, manned by a skinny clerk in his thirties.

"Yes, sir, can I help you?"

"So far, Clint was impressed by how polite everyone in this town had been.

"I need a room."

"Of course, sir," the man said. "If you'll just sign the register." He opened the book and set it in front of Clint, who signed it.

"Any idea how long you'll be with us?" the clerk asked.

"A couple of days, at least," Clint said.

"Here's your key, sir," the man said. "Top of the stairs and to the right, and then to the end of the hall. I hope you'll enjoy your stay."

"I hope so, too."

Considering his mood when he'd ridden in, things had gone pretty well, so far.

THREE

The room was satisfactory with a decent bed, a chest of drawers that was not in danger of falling apart, and a pitcher and basin that seemed clean enough. The window looked out over the main street and it was a sheer drop down, with no danger of anyone coming in through a window. As the years went by, more and more Clint had to be careful about the doors and windows of his hotel rooms. More than once bushwhackers had tried to kill him in his sleep because of who he was.

He dropped his saddlebags on the bed, propped his rifle nearby, and sat on the bed to take a breath.

*****

The boy Clint had given four bits to, Nathan, finished running his errand and then went to the three hotels in town to find out who the stranger with the big horse was. When he found out he ran home to tell his brothers.

The Tanner brothers did not have a good reputation in Casa Grande. Since the death of their parents they had continued to live in their house with their older sister, Julia, who was a hard worker. But the boys—Edward, 18, Sam, 17, and Nathan, 12—were more often than not in trouble. Julia, at 22, tried her hardest to be a substitute mother to them, but Ed and Sam made it very difficult.

Julia hoped that she'd be able to raise Nathan right, since he was only 12, but the young boy idolized his older brothers and was susceptible to their bad influence.

Nathan came running into the house, then stopped abruptly and looked around.

"Where's Julia?" he asked.

"Relax," Edward said, "she's working. You wanna run in the house, be my guest."

The three boys shared a room, which was crammed with three beds. At the moment Ed was reclining on his, and Sam was asleep on his. Whenever Julia wasn't home to nag them to do chores, they were more than likely asleep. If they were awake, they were trying to figure out ways to get into trouble. That was her opinion. They figured they were trying to come up with ways to make some money.

What Nathan didn't know was that Ed and Sam had recently gotten themselves into a lot of trouble—the worse ever—and were staying close to home until they could figure a way out.

"What're you so excited about?" Ed asked.

"Well," Nathan said, "for one thing I made six bits today."

Ed sat up in bed.

"Where is it?"

"In my pocket."

"Give it here."

"Aw, Ed—"

"You know the rules," Ed said. "We share."

Grudgingly, Nathan gave up his six bits. Ed gave two bits back to him, and put the other four in his pocket with a sly glance over at the sleeping Sam.

"I'll give Sam his when he wakes up." Ed looked at his little brother. "So what else are you excited about?"

"Well, I got the two bits from Mr. Willis at the General Store, just for deliverin' a message to his wife, but the four bits...I got that from the Gunsmith."

"What Gunsmith?" Ed scratched his head.

"The Gunsmith, Ed," Nathan said. "Clint Adams."

"What? You mean...*the* Gunsmith?"

"That's right!'

"What's he doin' in town?"

"His horse threw a shoe, and he had a broken boot heel," Nathan said. "He asked me if we had a cobbler in town."

"Is he stayin' in town?"

"He sure is."

"How do you know?"

"I checked the hotels," Nathan said. "He got a room at the Shrewsbury."

"That was good thinkin', little brother, to check the hotels," Ed said. "Where's his horse?"

"At the livery, I guess."

"Well, you go and find out for sure," Ed said.

"I tol' him if he needs anythin' else he should let me know."

"Did you tell him where ya live?"

"No, just my name."

"Well, if you see him again, don't tell him," Ed said. "I don't want him knowin' where we are."

"Okay, Ed."

"But you run now and find out where his horse is."

"Okay, Ed."

As Nathan was going out the door Ed shouted, "And if you see Julia, don't tell her nothin'."

"Right, Ed!"

As the younger brother ran off Ed turned and threw his pillow at his brother, Sam.

"Wake up, Sam!" he shouted.

"Wha—" Sam came awake, looked around, bleary-eyed. "What'dja say?"

"I said I got an idea," Ed said. "I know how we can make some big money."

"How?"

"Wake the hell up, and I'll tell ya!"

FOUR

Clint went down to the lobby, where the clerk was eager to help in any way he could.

"This seems like a nice, quiet town," Clint said.

"Oh, it is, sir," the clerk said. "Everybody here is very welcoming."

"Well, I'm interested in a good steak and a cold beer," Clint said. Those were pretty much the first things he looked for in every town he visited. And he'd learned long ago to ask where to find then, rather than having to wade through some rubbery steaks and warm beer.

"We have several places to eat, sir, and they're all good," the clerk said. "And either saloon has cold beer. You can't go wrong."

Clint frowned. The hostler had used those same exact words.

"Is that some sort of town slogan, or something?"

"Sir?"

"Never mind," Clint said. "Thanks for the...advice."

"Certainly, sir."

He went outside, stopped on the boardwalk to look around. It was afternoon, and people were out walking, going in and out of the stores, loading supplies on buckboards. There didn't seem to be anyone who wasn't doing something, no one leaned against a post having a smoke, or sitting in a chair whittling.

The place had an odd feel to it, but maybe he just hadn't encountered a lot of quiet towns where everyone seemed to be doing something productive.

He started walking, and stepped into the first café he came to. It had one large window, and on it was lettered the name MIRABELLA'S. He went inside.

Since most folks seemed to be out and about working he was able to take any table he wanted. He chose the one furthest from the door and window.

"What can I get you, sir?" the waiter asked, politely.

"Steak," Clint said, "and anything else you can fit on the plate. Do you serve beer?"

"Yes, sir."

"Cold beer."

"Comin' up, sir."

Clint wondered if he could get tired of so much polite behavior. Maybe he'd encounter something different—or normal—at a saloon.

*****

Nathan ran to the livery stable right from home, saw that Hoss was making a fuss over the big horse the Gunsmith had ridden into town on.

"Is that his horse?"

Hoss turned and looked at Nathan.

"Oh, hey, Nate. Whose horse?"

"The Gunsmith."

Hoss stopped brushing the horse and looked down at Nathan.

"That who he was?" he asked. "Come to think of it, he did say his name was Clint."

"Right, Clint Adams. He gave me four bits."

"That's a lot of money for a ten year old."

"I'm twelve," Nathan said, frowning.

"Really? Must be small for your age."

"Aw, Hoss," Nathan said, "as big as you are, everybody looks small for their age."

The big man laughed and said, "You're probably right, youngster. You better skedaddle. I told the man I'd take good care of his horse."

"Okay," Nathan said. "See ya, Hoss."

The big man waved, went back to brushing the big Darley Arabian.

Nathan left the livery, decided to try and find out where the Gunsmith was at that moment.

FIVE

The steak was good, not great; the beer cold, but not ice cold. Clint was finding out that what the town had in spades was manners, but nothing else was as good as the townspeople seemed to think it was.

He paid his bill and left the café. His next task was to find a saloon and see if the beer was ice cold there, and if the bartender was as polite as everyone else had been.

He came out the door and was immediately run into by someone.

"Whoa!" he said, catching the boy. Then he looked down and recognized the boy who had given him directions. "Well, hello. Nathan, isn't it?"

"Yessir." He looked up at Clint with wide eyes.

"Where are you off to in such a rush?"

"Nowhere, sir."

"You always rush when you're goin' nowhere?"

"Yessir," Nathan said. "My sister says I'm gonna run to my own grave if I ain't careful."

"Your sister, huh?"

'Yessir. She's real pretty. You'd like her. You wanna meet her?"

"Not right now, Nathan," Clint said. "Right now I'm about to rush off to find a cold beer."

"Hey, I can take ya," Nathan said, grabbing Clint's left arm. "I know where the beer's real cold."

"Is that a fact? Well, okay, then. Show me and I'll give you another two bits."

"Yessir!" Nathan said. "This way!"

*****

"You're crazy," Sam said to his brother.

"Am I?"

"We're in enough trouble as it is," Sam said, "and you wanna make it worse!"

"Not worse, Sam," Ed said. "Better."

"You think kidnappin's gonna make things better for us?" Sam asked. "Julia'll kill us!"

"Are you afraid of Julia, Sam?"

"Well...uh, no," Sam said.

"Then what's the problem?" Ed said. "Look, we owe the Colter Gang a lot of money, and if we don't pay 'em they're gonna kill us. Or worse, they'll go to Julia to get the money. You want Julia to find out what we done?"

"Hell, no!" Sam didn't want Ed to know it, but he was afraid of his older sister.

"Well, there you go, then," Ed said. "My idea is the answer. It's out only way out."

"B-but, how we gonna do it?" Sam asked.

"That's the smart part," Ed said. "We're gonna use Nate."

"Nate?" Sam asked. "How's our little brother gonna help us with a kidnappin'?"

"You just listen to my plan..."

*****

Nathan dragged Clint along the street, past people who stepped aside, smiling or laughing.

"Here ya go!" Nathan announced. "This here's the Purple Garter, and they got cold beer."

"How do you know that? You're only twelve."

"My brother told me."

"You have a brother?"

"I got two."

"You've got two brothers, and a sister?"

"Yessir."

"All older?"

"Yessir."

"You've got a big family. What about your parents."

"They're dead."

"Both of them?"

"Yessir."

"So your brothers take care of you?"

"My sister takes care of all of us," Nathan said. "She's the oldest."

"I see. Well, here you go." Instead of giving the boy two bits he gave him a dollar.

"Wow!"

"Don't spend that all in one place."

"I can't spend it at all, sir," Nathan said. "I gotta share it with my brothers."

"Sounds like you've got a good relationship with your brothers," Clint said.

"Yessir. Real good."

"Well, you take care, Nathan," Clint said, "and thanks."

Clint entered the Purple Garter and found it, even in the afternoon, fairly busy. On his way to the bar he heard one argument and saw one fight almost start, and thought maybe he'd found someplace a little more normal in this polite town.

At the bar the big bartender looked at him sourly and said, "What'll ya have?"

"Beer," Clint said. "I have it on good authority that you serve it cold."

"Ice cold," the bartender said. "Who tol' ya?"

"A boy named Nathan."

"Nate's a good kid," the man said, setting a beer in front of him.

Clint heard somebody yell, turned to look, saw a couple of men shoving each other.

"It doesn't seem as polite in here as it does all over town," Clint said.

"You just ride in?"

"This morning."

"We got a new mayor," the bartender said. "He ran on a reform ticket, said he was gonna change everything in town. Well, he done it. He changed everything but this place. He even tried to get us to change the name."

"What's wrong with the Purple Garter?"

"He said it gave folks the wrong idea," the bartender said. "What kinda wrong idea? Men come here to drink, gamble, argue, fight-"

"No women?" Clint asked, looking around.

The bartender got a sour look on his face.

"That mayor, he managed to change that. He outlawed what he called 'scarlet women' in town."

"No saloon girls?"

"No saloon girls, no whorehouse, no nothin'," the bartender said.

Clint sipped the beer and was pleasantly surprised.

"At least you've still got cold beer."

"Yeah," the bartender said, "at least he ain't outlawed that!"

SIX

The Purple Garter made Clint relax. Even though there were no girls, the place felt like home to anyone who enjoyed spending time in saloons.

Finally, as he was working his way through his beer, a fight did break out in the back of the room.

"What do you do about that?" Clint asked the bartender.

"That? That's just a couple of boys blowin' off steam. Everybody's tip-toein' around out there, they gotta blow off steam someplace."

"What about the sheriff? Does he get called in here?"

"He stays away," the barman said, "only comes if there's shots."

"So he goes along with the mayor."

"The whole town council goes along with the Mayor," the bartender said. "The sheriff wants to keep his job."

"What about you?" Clint asked. "You on the town council?"

The bartender looked at him.

"What makes you think I own this place?"

Clint looked at the purple garter on the man's right sleeve and said, "Call it a hunch."

"Well, let's just say I was on the council, but the Mayor and me, we don't see eye-to-eye, so I was asked to leave. 'nother beer?'

"Sure."

The bartender took the empty mug and refilled it.

"What brings you to town?"

"Broken heel on my boot, thrown shoes on my horse," Clint said. "Then I thought I'd stick around a couple of days and take it easy."

"Well, if that's all yer lookin' for you came to the right place," the man said. "But if yer lookin' for any action—poker, girls, whatever—let me know."

"I will," Clint said. "Thanks."

"My name's Big Bill," the bartender said.

"Clint."

"Enjoy yer beer, Clint."

As the barman drifted away, Clint wondered if the word had gotten around town yet that he was there. Did the bartender know who he was? He didn't think so.

But somebody did. He was halfway through his second beer when the batwings opened and a man wearing a badge walked in. The bartender had said the Sheriff stayed away. Clint could only think of one thing that might have brought the man there.

It got quiet in the place for a minute, and then slowly the conversation started up again. The sheriff walked to the bar, took a place a few feet to Clint's right.

"I get a beer, Bill?" he asked. He was a tall, rangy man in his thirties, wearing freshly cleaned clothes. Looked like the Mayor liked his lawmen clean.

Bill set a beer in front of him and said, "What brings you in, Sheriff? I didn't hear any shots here."

"Not yet, maybe," the lawman said. He looked down at Clint. "I heard this fella here was in town and thought I'd pay a little visit. I knew it wouldn't be long till he found his way here."

"He ain't doin' nothin' but drinkin' beer, Sheriff," the bartender said. "I can testify to that."

"You know who this fella is?" the Sheriff asked.

"Says his name is Clint."

"Adams," the sheriff said. "Clint Adams."

"That right?" Bill asked. "The Gunsmith?"

"That's right."

Bill looked down at Clint, who couldn't hear them from where he was standing.

"Well, he don't look like he's lookin' fer trouble, does he?"

"He don't have to look for trouble, Bill," the sheriff said. "Trouble pretty much looks for men like him."

"Well, not so far."

"Well," the sheriff said, picking up his beer, "let's see what the man has to say for himself."

SEVEN

lint couldn't hear the conversation between the sheriff and the bartender, but he could guess. And when the lawman picked up his beer and started for him, he knew he was right. He picked up his own beer and waited.

"Mr. Adams?" the lawman asked.

"That's right."

"My name's Gregorius," the man told him. "Sheriff Tom Gregorius."

"Nice to meet you, Sheriff. What's on your mind?"

"Well, not having any trouble in my town, that's always on my mind."

"Well, that's on my mind too, Sheriff."

"Glad to hear it," Gregorius said. "I heard your horse threw a shoe."

"That's right, but I'm getting it fixed."

"Figure on leaving town once that's done?"

"I actually figured on staying around a day or two," Clint said. "You got an unusually quiet town."

"And we like it that way."

"I can see why," Clint said. "It doesn't leave much for you to do."

There was a crash from the back of the room, like somebody broke a chair, but the Sheriff did not even give it a look.

"I kind of like it that way," Gregorius said, "but that don't mean I can't handle anything that might come along."

"I'm sure you can handle things in a very competent and...clean manner, Sheriff."

The man was rubbing Clint the wrong way, which was why he made the "clean" remark.

The sheriff laughed.

"Yeah, I like to keep clean," he said. "My clothes and my gun, so my advice to you is not to do anything that's going to make me have to get dirty."

"I didn't ride in looking for trouble, Sheriff," Clint said. "In fact, I didn't even ride in, I walked."

"I heard."

Clint figured it was either the hostler or the hotel desk clerk who had given him up to the lawman. He didn't mind. Whichever it was, he was probably just doing what they had all been told to do.

The sheriff finished his beer, looked at Clint's mug, turned, and said, "Hey Bill, give our guest another one on my tab, huh?"

"Sure thing, Sheriff."

"Mr. Adams," the Sheriff said.

"Sheriff," Clint said, "thanks."

As the lawman left, the bartender brought a fresh beer over to Clint.

"His tab," the barman said, with distaste. "That man hasn't paid for a drink since he put on that badge a year ago."

"No problem," Clint said, and dropped some money on the bar. "I pay my own way."

Bill didn't argue, he just picked up the money.

"That when the mayor took office, too?"

"Yep."

"So you've got to put up with him for at least what? Three more years?"

"Maybe more," the bartender said. "He figures to get reelected if things stay as quiet as they been. The shopkeepers like it, and so do their wives. Especially since they don't have to worry about their husbands goin' to a whorehouse to see some girls."

"Unless they come to see you first, right?"

The bartender grinned tightly.

"I do what I can to keep spirits up around here."

"Mind if I ask about the purple garter?"

"This place used to be called the Broken Wheel," he said, "but when the Mayor took office I changed it to the Purple Garter."

"Just to get his goat?"

"That's right."

Clint raised his glass in a salute and said, "I like it."

*****

In the back of the room the argument that had resulted in a broken chair was going on between two members of the Colter Gang. Other patrons around them were trying to keep out of the way, so that the gang members wouldn't turn their anger on them, instead. The secret hope among men in the saloon was that the Colter Gang would shoot each other.

But that wasn't going to happen as long as Ken Colter was sitting there with them. His men knew that any arguments among themselves had to be settled with no gunplay, otherwise they'd have to face a Colter gun—not Ken's, but his brother Greg. The youngest of the three brothers, Greg was in his late twenties, and was wicked fast with a handgun.

But even the Colters confined their arguments to the confines of the Purple Garter. That was because Ken had a working relationship with the mayor that kept the sheriff off their backs, as long as they didn't cause any trouble within the town limits.

The middle brother, Jerry, came back to the table with beers for him and his brothers, sat down next to Ken, and said, "I got news."

"What news?"

"There's a fella in town you might not want Greg to know about."

"Yeah?" Ken picked up the fresh beer. "Who's that?"

"Clint Adams."

Ken stopped with the beer halfway to his mouth. He looked across the table at Greg, who was watching the two arguing gang members with a smile on his face.

"Are you serious?"

"Yup."

"Where is he?"

"At the bar, talking to the sheriff."

"So that's what Johnny Law is doin' in here," Ken said. "I was wonderin'."

Jerry drank some beer.

"You know if Greg hears he's here, he's gonna wanna try him."

Ken thought a moment, then said, "Greg's pretty fast. That might be interestin'."

"But you promised the mayor—"

"I know what I promised the mayor," Ken said, cutting his brother off. "All I said was, it would be interestin'." He drank some more beer. "Yes, sir, mighty interesting."

EIGHT

Sam still thought his brother was crazy, but he was also coming around to Ed's way of thinking.

They were sitting out in front of their house, sharing a bottle of whiskey they had stolen from the General Store, passing it back and forth.

"How do we do it?" Sam asked.

"We use Nathan."

"Nathan!" Sam said. "He's twelve."

"He's trustworthy," Ed said. "Are we?"

"You got a point," Sam said, "but if Julia finds out—"

"Sam," Ed said, "you got to stop bein' afraid of Julia. She's just a girl."

"I know, I know." He passed the bottle back to his brother. "So where do we take 'im after we grab him? Not here."

"Hell no, not here!" Ed said. "We don't need to deal with Julia."

"But you ain't afraid of her."

"I ain't," Ed said, "but we don't need her stickin' her nose in our business, either, do we?"

"No, sir!" He took the bottle back. "So how do we get Nathan to help?"

"That's easy," Ed said. "We stop treatin' him like a kid."

*****

Gloria Knight spent the day thinking about the man she'd met at the cobbler's.

"Ma'am?"

She jerked her head up, saw that Julia Tanner was looking at her, and realized that Julia had called out her name several times.

"Oh, I'm sorry, Julia," Gloria said. "I don't know where my mind is."

Julia smiled and asked, "Is it a man?"

"What?"

"You met a man today."

"I—what? I don't know what you mean." Gloria hoped she wasn't blushing.

"I'm just guessing, Gloria," Julia said. "When I can't concentrate, it's usually because of a boy—I mean, a man." Julia was very aware of the fact that she was 22 and should not be concerned with boys anymore. If she didn't find a man soon, she was going to be an old maid.

Being unmarried did not seem to bother Gloria Knight, and Julia admired her for that. She knew that Gloria had been married when she was Julia's age, but her husband had died several years later and she had never married again. Did her marriage early in life keep her from actually being an old maid now? Was that why it didn't bother her? Julia never asked, because she liked the woman very much, and didn't want to hurt her feelings.

"I'm sorry," she said. "I shouldn't have said anything."

"No, no,'" Gloria said, "it's all right. Did you have something you wanted to ask me?"

"Just about Mrs. Kennely's dress," Julia said. "Pearl buttons, was it?"

"Yes, Julia, that's correct," Gloria said, "pearl buttons."

"Yes, Ma'am."

Julia returned to the rear of the shop, where she had been working on Mrs. Kennely's new dress.

Gloria Knight touched her face. Julia was very smart and dependable, so much unlike her brothers, Ed and Sam. Nathan, only 12, had time to turn out right, but those two, they were turning out badly.

Gloria decided to do her best to stop thinking about the man she'd met earlier in the day and get some work done.

NINE

It was dusk when Clint left the Purple Garter. Time to eat again, even though he'd had a full steak dinner for lunch.

He walked the streets, exchanging greetings with the polite citizens, finally came to another restaurant, different than the one he'd eaten in earlier. He went inside, found most of the tables full. In fact, they were all full.

He was starting to think he'd have to go elsewhere when he saw a familiar face, and she saw him. She smiled and waved at him to come over.

"I have an empty seat here, if you like," Gloria Knight said, "unless you'd rather wait?"

"No," he said. "I'll sit. Thank you."

"As you can see, I haven't been served yet, so you have time to order and we can eat together."

"That sounds good."

The waiter came over and Gloria said, "Please take my guest's order."

"Yes, Madam."

"Do you have beef stew?" Clint asked.

"Yes, sir."

"I'll have that."

"Fine choice, sir. And to drink?"

"Beer."

"Coming up."

The man left to fill the order.

"He's very good," Clint said. "Local?"

"No," she said, "he's from San Francisco. He decided to come West to make his fortune, and ended up still being a waiter. But a good one."

The waiter brought beer for Clint and a cup of coffee for Gloria.

"How was your day?" she asked. "Did you see much of the town?"

"I saw the inside of the Purple Garter."

"Ah," she said, with a smile, "the bane of the Ladies League, and the mayor."

"Why doesn't he close it down?"

"The mayor has gotten most of the town to toe the line," she said. "If he took the Purple Garter away from the men in town, where would they blow off steam? The streets."

"So he figures it's a necessary evil?"

"Apparently."

"What do you think of the way things are in this town?" he asked.

"Frankly?"

"Please."

"I think eventually the town is going to explode," she said. "I just don't have any idea when."

"Sounds like a very honest opinion," Clint said. "To me, the people in this town look like they're sleep walking. The only place that feels normal is the Purple Garter."

The waiter came then with their meals, and he saw that Gloria had ordered a roast chicken dinner, which featured only a quarter of a chicken and some vegetables. His own bowl of beef stew was filled almost to overflowing and was accompanied by some crusty bread.

"Thank you, Arthur," Gloria said.

Yes, thank you," Clint echoed.

"Enjoy your meals, folks."

As they ate she asked, "Did you get your horse shoed?"

"I did," he said.

"So does that mean you'll be leaving town, uh, soon?"

"No," he said, "not soon. I might stay around a day or two."

"Oh? Why's that?"

"Well," he said, "the town is quiet, the people are polite, and my horse and I do need some rest."

"How nice," she said. "Maybe we'll get to see each other again."

"Well," he said, "we're not finished seeing each other this evening, are we?"

"No," she agreed, "we're not."

*****

Gloria told Clint about her background. Having been born in a nearby smaller town she went East to be educated and upon returning found her town gone. So she moved to Casa Grande and opened her store, at first calling it a dress shop, but then changing it to a "boutique".

"It's French," she said.

"And what does it mean?" he asked.

"Oh, it just means a small store selling, uh, dresses," she said, "but it sounds better, doesn't it?"

"Much better. Do you work in the store alone?"

"No, I usually have a helper. I've had several, but the one I have now—Julia Tanner—shows real promise. She'll be a very good dressmaker one day. I wish I could get her to go East to school."

"Is she too young?"

"No, quite the contrary, she's too old," Gloria said. "Oh, I don't mean she's old. She's twenty-two. The problem is her brothers."

"Ah..."

"She says she can't leave them."

"How old are they?"

"Um, I think they're eighteen and seventeen, but Nathan, he's only twelve."

"I know Nathan."

"You do?"

He nodded. "I met him when I first came to town. He gave me directions."

"Did you pay him?"

"Of course. I gave him four bits."

"His brothers probably took it away from him," she said. "They're bad boys."

"How bad?"

"Getting worse as they get older," she said. "I'm sure they'll eventually be outlaws. But Julia thinks she can keep them in line. That's what keeps her here."

"Where are the parents?"

"Dead."

"The girl sounds very responsible."

"She is," Gloria said, "but it's going to ruin her life."

"That's too bad."

When they were finished with desert Gloria tried to pay the check, but Clint wouldn't allow it.

"I invited you," she insisted.

"To share your table," he said. "You didn't offer to buy my meal."

He paid the bill and they left the restaurant.

"Can I walk you home?" he asked.

"You know this is a very quiet town, right?" she said. "I'll be quite safe."

"Just an excuse to share your company a little longer," he admitted.

She blushed prettily and said, "Well then, how can I refuse?"

TEN

Gloria had a small house just on the outskirts of town. They strolled there, passing only a few people as the town was starting to settle down for the evening.

"Most of the stores close by four," she explained.

"Aren't there people who need to do business after that?" he asked.

"Some," she said. "They have to make special arrangements. Tell me, who else have you met in town?"

"Well, aside from some waiters and a hotel clerk, I met the sheriff."

"Oh." There was no inflection in the word.

"What does that mean?"

"Oh, nothing much," she said.

"Do you know him?"

"Of course."

"What do you think of him?"

"Oh," she said, "nothing much."

"That was the impression I got."

"I don't like to say anything bad about people," she said. "So if I can't say something nice, I try not to say anything at all."

"That's a good policy."

They walked a while longer, Gloria simply pointing out things she thought might be of interest to him - they weren't - when he asked, "As a business owner, are you on the town council?"

"Oh, no," she said, firmly.

"Why not?"

"Well, there are several reasons. One is, I'm a small business owner. The members of the council all own large businesses in town."

"And?"

"And I'm a woman," she said. "They don't want a woman to have a seat."

"Is that all?"

"No," she said, "but remember what I said a few minutes ago? About not saying anything if I couldn't say something nice?"

"Yes," he said, "I remember that."

"Let's just leave it at that, then," she suggested.

He laughed and said, "Okay, fine. I won't push you."

"This is my house."

It was a small wood frame house that looked well cared for, with a small garden surrounded by a fence to keep critters out.

"It's nice," he said.

"And comfortable," she said. "Inside, I mean."

"I understand."

"I would invite you in, but..."

"It wouldn't look good."

"No, no," she said, "it's only that we've just met and—"

"You don't know me very well."

"Not so much that," she said, "but I'm afraid I didn't clean up very well this morning before I went to work."

"Oh, so after you've cleaned up you'll invite me in?" he asked. "For a cup of coffee or something?"

"Yes," she said, "I will."

"Like, next time?"

"Next time what?"

"Next time we share a meal," he said, "or see each other."

"Will we be sharing another meal?" she asked.

"I hope so."

"Then yes," she said, "definitely, next time."

"Maybe," he said, "I'll come by and see your shop."

"Oh, why would you do that?" she asked. "What interest would you have in a dress shop?"

"None," he admitted, "but I might be interested in seeing a boutique."

She smiled, said, Goodnight," and he watched her until she was inside her house.

ELEVEN

When Julia got home she knew her brothers were up to something.

"You're both here," she said.

"Where would we be?" Ed asked.

"Out making trouble."

"For who?"

"What does it matter?" she asked. "Somebody."

Ed looked at Sam, who looked away.

"We're just here waiting for our supper, Julia," Ed told her.

"Where's Nathan?"

"He'll be here," Ed said. "He's twelve. He gets hungry."

"I'll have dinner ready in half an hour," she said. "Why don't you go out and find Nathan?"

"Sure. Come on, Sam."

"And do it without getting into trouble," she said.

Ed spread his hands and said, "We ain't gonna look for no trouble, Julia. We never do."

"Maybe not," Julia said. "But it's amazing how trouble just seems to find you two."

"I don't know what you're talkin' about, sis," Ed said. "Come, Sam, let's find Nathan."

They left the house, and Julia set about to make supper for her family.

Those two were up to something.

*****

"She knows," Sam said.

"Knows what?"

"That we're plannin' somethin'," Sam said. "She always knows."

When they were far enough away from the house not to be seen, Ed stopped walking and leaned against a tree.

"What are you doin'?" Sam asked. "I thought we were gonna look for Nathan."

"He'll come home when he gets hungry."

"She's gonna get mad, Ed."

"Let 'er get mad, Sam," Ed said, "and no, she don't know nothin'. Maybe she thinks we're up to somethin', but she always thinks that."

"That's because we're always up to somethin', Ed," Sam admitted.

"Yeah, but she don't know what," Ed said, "and she ain't gonna. Just relax."

Sam looked around nervously. They were just outside of town, and if it wasn't dark they would have been able to see it. If it was earlier they'd have been able to hear people's voices.

"I think we should look for Nathan," Sam said.

"Why?"

"Because we're gonna need him for the plan, right?" Sam asked. "We gotta talk to him where Julia can't hear us."

"Well, Sam," Ed said, pushing away from the tree and standing up, "you just said somethin' smart."

"I did?"

"Yeah, you did," Ed said. He poked his brother in the chest. "Don't make a habit of it, or I'll die of shock."

"Aw, Ed—"

"Come on," Ed said, "let's find our little brother and see if we can do it without running into anybody from the Colter gang."

"Ah, geez..." Sam said. "I forgot about them. Maybe we oughtta stay here—"

Ed grabbed the front of his brother's shirt, pulled him along and said, "Come on!"

*****

Clint walked back to town, wondering if he should have tried harder to get invited into Gloria's house. Maybe not. She was, after all, a lady. He had to respect that.

As he walked past the Purple Garter he heard some noise from inside, decided it was too early to go to bed. Mighty as well go in, have a beer, and see what all the fuss was about.

As he entered he heard the sound of a breaking chair, saw the bartender standing behind the bar, shaking his head.

"Sounds like you're losing some furniture," Clint said, approaching the bar.

"Good thing I got extra in the back," Big Bill said. "You come back for another beer?"

"I did."

"Comin' up."

Big Bill drew a cold one for Clint and set it in front of him.

"You ain't lookin' for anythin' else, are ya?"

"Like what?"

"Like maybe some time with a gal?"

"For money?"

"Well, not for free," the man said.

"Sorry," Clint said, "I don't pay for those pleasures."

"Ever?"

"Nope," Clint said. "Never."

"What about a poker game?"

"High stakes?"

"Naw, not around here," Big Bill said. "Ain't nobody got the money for high stakes. Not anybody who comes in here, anyway."

"Then no, thanks," Clint said. "I'll just nurse my beer and listen to the furniture break."

"A couple more and I'm gonna have ta do somethin' to stop it."

"Well," Clint said, "let me know if you need any help."

"Sure," Big Bill said, "thanks."

TWELVE

Ed and Sam found Nathan peering underneath the batwing doors of the Purple Garter.

"Whatta ya think yer doin'?" Ed asked, grabbing him by the collar.

"I was just lookin'!"

"For what?" Sam said. "Some girl's titty?" He and Ed laughed.

"Naw," Nathan said, "I seen that already."

"You have?" Ed asked. "Where've you seen a girl's titty?"

"At home," Nathan said. "Walked in on Julia once when she was takin' a bath."

"Oh Lord," Sam said, putting his hands over his ears, "I ain't gonna be able to unhear that, or get it outta my head."

"What's wrong?" Nathan said. "She's got right nice titties."

"I'll bet she does," Ed said. "Wouldn't mind seein' those myself."

"Hey," Sam said, "that's our sister!"

"So what?" Ed asked. "She's got 'em, ain't she?"

"Pretty ones," Nathan said. "All pale with pink tips—"

"Shut up!" Sam said.

"Besides," Ed said, "how would you know a pretty one from an ugly one?"

"I dunno," Nathan said, sticking his chin out, "but they was pretty, is all I'm sayin'."

"Never mind," Ed said, releasing Nathan's collar. "What was you lookin at?"

"The Gunsmith's in there," Nathan said. "I thought he might shoot somebody."

"Where is he?" Ed asked.

"At the bar, talkin' ta Big Bill."

Ed peered over the batwings into the saloon.

"Standin' at the end of the bar?" he asked.

Nathan peeked under and said, "That's him."

"Take a look, Sam," Ed said.

Sam looked over the batwings.

"See 'im?" Ed asked.

"Yeah."

"Okay," Ed said. "Remember what he looks like."

"Okay."

"And now," Ed said, grabbing Nathan's collar again, "let's get home. Julia's makin' supper."

"What's she makin'?"

"I dunno, but she told us to find you, and that's what we done. Now let's go."

As they started walking back toward their house Nathan said, "Ed?"

"Yeah, what?"

"Why'd you tell Sam to remember what the Gun-smith looks like?"

"Never you mind, " Ed said, slapping the back of Nathan's head. "You just walk!"

*****

Julia looked out the front door for the hundredth time. Those boys should've been back with Nathan by now. Dinner was ready, so she decided to just put it on the table and they could all eat it cold if they didn't get back while it was still hot.

Or if they hadn't already got themselves—and poor Nathan—into trouble.

*****

There wasn't any more broken furniture in the Purple Garter, just some raised voices.

Clint had a second beer before deciding to go back to his hotel.

"Who's causing all that ruckus back there, anyway?" he asked, before leaving.

"That'd be the Colter boys."

"Who are they?"

"Local gang, gets themselves into trouble," Big Bill said. "If you believe what they say, they've been robbin' banks and stages all over the state."

"Wanted?"

"Not that I know of," Big Bill said, "but they'd like it if they were. It would mean they were successful."

"How many of them?"

"Here three brothers, several other members."

"Well, I never heard of them," Clint said.

"Just as well," the bartender said. "The younger one, Greg, fancies himself a fast gun. If he knew you were here he'd be all up in your face, tryin' to get you to draw on him.

"That wouldn't be a good idea," Clint said.

"For you or him?"

"Him." Clint dropped some money on the bar for the beer he drank and said, "'night."

"See ya tomorrow, if you're still around."

"I should be around," Clint said, "at least until tomorrow."

As he went out the batwings and stepped off the boardwalk he thought her heard another chair break.

*****

Greg Colter watched the fight, pleased that for once he wasn't involved. That meant he wasn't going to have to take any shit from his brothers.

He turned his head as somebody sat down across from him with a bottle of whiskey.

"About time," he said to Mickey Diggs, his best friend.

"I got news," Diggs said.

"Pour the drinks first."

Diggs opened the bottle and poured two glasses. Greg picked his up.

"Okay, what news."

"Clint Adams."

"What about him?"

"He's in town."

"What? Where?"

"Well," Diggs said, "up to five minutes ago he was standing at the bar."

Greg put his drink down and turned around to look.

"He's gone now."

"Why didn't you tell me right away?"

"I told you as soon as I got back to the table."

"Stay here."

Greg stood up, walked over to the table his brothers were sitting at.

"Did you two know Clint Adams was in town?"

Ken and Jerry looked at each other, and then Jerry looked away.

"Now look—" Ken said.

"You did know!" Greg said. "And you didn't tell me."

"Greg, listen—"

"I'm gonna kill 'im!" Greg said.

"Shut up a minute!" Ken snapped.

Greg fell silent with a wounded look.

"You wanna make a try for the Gunsmith, be my guest," Ken said. "I even think you have a chance at beating him."

"Okay then—"

"—only you have to do it somewhere else," Ken went on, "not here in Casa Grande."

"So we grab him and take him somewhere else."

"That can be arranged," Ken said. "Just relax and give me some time to think about it. Go back to your friend Diggs and stay out of trouble."

Greg stood.

"When do we do this?" he asked.

"Don't worry, Greg," Ken said. "Jerry and I will tell you when."

THIRTEEN

The growling of Clint's stomach woke him in the morning. He washed and dressed quickly and went out onto the street. Casa Grande was a busy place at eight a.m., the streets filled with people and traffic. He crossed the street, avoiding two horses and a team pulling a buckboard, and walked to the café he'd eaten at when he first got to town the day before, only because it was closer.

The place was half filled, but he found a table he was comfortable with and ordered steak and eggs and a pot of coffee.

"Strong," he said. "Make the coffee strong."

"Okay," the waiter said.

Clint looked around, saw most of the tables were taken up by townspeople, merchants mostly sitting in twos and threes. A couple of tables had couples, and one had a family, two parents and two kids, a boy and a girl. The children seemed very curious about Clint, who smiled at them. They quickly looked shyly away.

Some of the adults stole glances at him, and he assumed that the word has gone out that he was in town. It was something he had no control over wherever he went.

His breakfast came and he attacked it, wondering what it was about the town, or the weather, that had made him so ravenous this morning.

He was halfway through his breakfast when Sheriff Gregorius walked in. At first Clint thought he was just there for breakfast, but then the man spotted him and walked over to him.

"Looking for me, Sheriff?"

"Actually," Gregorius said, "I was just coming in for breakfast, but when I saw you I thought, why not join you? Do you mind?"

"No, I don't mind at all."

The Sheriff sat down, looked at Clint's plate, and said, "That looks good."

"It is."

"'mornin', Sheriff," the waiter said. "The usual?"

"No," the lawman said, "I'll have the same as my friend here."

"Comin' up."

"And bring another pot of coffee, please," Clint said.

"Yes, sir."

"Well," the Sheriff said, "how was your night at the Purple Garter?"

"I had a few beers and went to my hotel room."

"Exciting night, then?"

"Lots of Mark Twain."

"Who?"

"Never mind. How's your mayor doing?"

"The mayor?"

"I hear he made some big changes when he took over."

"Changes for the better," the lawman said. "Got rid of a lot of the negative influences in town."

"Negative influences?" Clint repeated. "That sounds like politician talk."

"Whatever it is, it worked."

"Like getting rid of the whorehouse?"

"First thing he did."

"And that's all right with you?"

"To tell you the truth, I coulda gone either way," Gregorius said, "but it made the women in town—especially the married ones—very happy."

"Yeah, it would. But I see he didn't go so far as to close the saloons."

"Well," the lawman said, "he knew that would've been silly. Changed the names, though, got rid of the girls and most of the gambling."

"Except for the Purple Garter."

"Well," the sheriff said, "that place was pretty popular. Still is. Lots of men go there to blow off steam. Causes less trouble if they keep that sort of thing to one place."

"Makes your job easier, huh?"

"Definitely."

The waiter came with the Sheriff's plate and another pot of coffee.

"Wow," Gregorius said, after sipping, "that's strong."

"Only way to drink it," Clint said.

The lawman cut into his steak and asked, "So what are your plans for today?"

"Keeping track of me?"

"Just doing my job."

"Well, Sheriff," Clint said, "I intend to spend the day staying out of trouble."

"Mr. Adams," the sheriff said, "that sounds a lot like you'll be doin' my job for me."

*****

When they finished breakfast they left the café together, stopping just outside.

"I suppose you'll be off to make your rounds," Clint said.

"Tryin' to get rid of me?"

"Yes."

The lawman must have thought he was kidding, because he laughed.

"Do you have any deputies?" Clint asked.

"No need," the Sheriff said. "I did have two, but when the new mayor took over he had me let them go. Save the town some money."

"Of course."

"No, no," Gregorius said, "it worked out just fine, actually. Most of the trouble we've had this past year I've been able to handle myself. If I need help, I draft somebody temporarily."

"Whatever works for you, I guess."

"Enjoy your day, Mr. Adams," the sheriff said. "If there's anythin' I can do for you, let me know."

"Right, thanks."

The sheriff started to walk away, then turned back and said, "Oh, and remember—"

"Stay out of trouble," Clint said. "I've got it, Sheriff."

The lawman smiled and walked away.

FOURTEEN

"So you wanna meet him?" Nathan asked his brother.

"That's right," Ed said. "Sam and me wanna meet 'im. And you're friends with him, right?"

"That's right!"

"So you can arrange it fer us," Ed said, slapping his little brother on the shoulder.

They'd had breakfast, prepared for them by Julia before she left for her job. Once she was gone, Ed knew he could talk Nathan into helping them with their plan to kidnap Clint Adams, the Gunsmith.

"I can do that," Nathan said, proud of his friendship with the famous man.

"Okay," Ed said. "You know that corral behind the livery down on First Street?"

"Yeah, I know it."

"See if you can get him to meet you there around noon."

"Why there?" Nathan asked, scrunching up his face.

"It's out of the way," Ed said. "We don't wanna share our time with the Gunsmith with anybody else, do we?"

"We sure don't!" Nathan said.

"Off you go, then," Ed said. "He's probably havin' breakfast right about now. I'll bet you can catch him right on Main Street."

"Okay," Nathan said, heading for the door.

"Make sure you come back and tell us it's arranged," Ed said.

"I'll be back," Nathan promised and ran out the door.

"Whatta ya think he's gonna do when he finds out what we done?" Sam asked.

"Don't worry about him," Ed said. "Once we give him his share of the ransom., he'll be fine."

They sat back down at the kitchen table.

"How much ransom do you think we should ask for?" Sam asked.

"A lot," Ed said.

"Like a thousand dollars?"

"That ain't a lot!" Ed scolded his brother. "Yer such a small thinker, Sam. That's why you gotta leave the thinkin' to me."

"So how much, then?"

"I dunno," Ed said. "Maybe...five thousand. Yeah. Five thousand dollars. That's a lot of money."

"It sure is," Sam said, his eyes wide. "With five thousand dollars, we'd be rich!"

Ed frowned. With five thousand dollars he'd be rich, but not if he had to share the money with Sam, Nathan, and Julia.

He was having second thoughts about how much to ask for, and it so occupied his thoughts that he never once asked himself the obvious question.

FIFTEEN

Nathan saw that his big brother Ed was right. He got to Main Street just in time to see Clint Adams come out of the café with the sheriff. He frowned, wondering if the sheriff was trying to arrest the Gunsmith. As he watched they talked, and then the sheriff walked away, smiling. Nathan heaved a sigh of relief, and hurried across the street to the Gunsmith...

"Hey, Mr. Adams!" he yelled.

Clint turned at the sound of his name, saw young Nathan hurrying his way.

"Hey, Nathan," Clint said. "Slow down."

"I been lookin' for ya."

"Well, you found me," Clint said. "What's on your mind?"

"My brothers wanna meet ya."

"Is that so?"

"I said I could arrange it, us bein' friends, and all," Nathan said. "Um, we are friends, ain't we?"

"Yes, we are."

"Then you'll come and meet them?"

"Sure I will. Where are they?"

"They're gonna be behind the livery stable at noon," Nathan said. "That way nobody'll see us and we won't have to introduce you to anybody else."

"Well, that's good," Clint said. "I can check on my horse at the same time."

"Well, I gotta go run some errands for my sister," Nathan said. "She told me this mornin' she needed me, and that Miss Knight would pay me."

"Well, why don't I walk over there with you," Clint suggested. "I've met Miss Knight, but I haven't met your sister."

"Okay! Let's go!"

*****

Greg Colter rolled over in bed and bumped into the naked girl sleeping next to him. He frowned, then remembered. In order to take his mind off killing the Gunsmith his brothers had bought him a girl last night. The Purple Garter was the only place in town you could do that, and the room he was in was right upstairs.

He propped himself up on one elbow and studied her. She had long red hair and pale skin, with freckles here and there. He couldn't see her breasts because she was lying on her stomach, but he remembered she had a lot of freckles in between them.

She turned her head toward him and opened one green eye.

"Like what you see?" she asked.

"I sure do." He reached out, traced the line of her back down to the little indentation just above her buttocks, then ran his hand over both of the smooth globes, in turn.

"Well, it's all yours," she said, "until noon, then I'm back on my own time, so..." she rolled over onto her back and put her hands up over her head, ". . . how do you want me?"

There were all those freckles between her small breasts, and that bush between her legs was just a little deeper red than the hair on her head.

"Just like that will be fine," he said. He ran his hand down the front of her body, then poked his fingers into that red bush. All he had to do was touch her and she got wet right away. He was able to slide his middle finger into her easily and she groaned as he slid it in and out a few times.

"Oh, baby," she said, "that's it, just like that ..." She thought, what a dummy. Her whore talk was getting him all excited, and she couldn't wait for him to climb on top of her, stick it in, and finish so she could go and get some breakfast.

"Come on, baby," she said, "time for you to stick it in me."

"You asked for it," he said.

He climbed atop her, poked at her a few times, until she finally reached between them took hold of him and guided him into her.

"Fuck me, baby," she said, and thought, come on, get it over with.

SIXTEEN

Clint followed Nathan into Gloria Knight's "boutique," although it looked suspiciously like a dress shop to him.

"Hi, Julia!" Nathan shouted.

A young girl turned to look at him. When she saw Clint her eyes went wide. She was a beauty, blonde and blue-eyed, with a trim figure that was full in the bust.

"This is my friend, Clint Adams," Nathan said. "He's the Gunsmith."

"Oh, well, hello, Mr. Adams," Julia said. "You're...a gunsmith?"

"He's the Gunsmith," Nathan said. "He's famous, Julia."

"Oh, well..."

At that moment Gloria Knight came walking out from a back room, stopped short when she saw him.

"Oh, Clint!" she said. "How nice."

"I told you I'd be coming by to see your shop," Clint said, "and when my friend Nathan said his sister worked here and he had to come and see her, I just figured I'd walk over with him."

"This is it, then," she said, spreading her arms. "It's a little cluttered because we're filling some orders."

"And Julia is your only employee?"

"Oh, yes," Gloria said. "I started out training her, but she's turned into quite a seamstress."

"Which means," Julia said, "I should be getting back to work. I was only watching the front of the store while Gloria was in the back. Nathan, come in the back with me. I have some things for you to do."

Nathan looked at Clint.

"I told you she had work for me," he said. "See you at noon?"

"I'll see you at noon," Clint promised.

"Nathan," Julia said, as she walked to the back of the store, "come along. It was nice meeting you, Mr. Adams."

"Nice to meet you, too, Julia."

When they were gone Gloria moved in behind the counter.

"She's a wonderful worker," she said, "and a great girl. And I'm sure you've noticed what a beauty she is."

"Yes," he said, "quite beautiful."

"It's too bad about those brothers. What's happening with you and Nathan at noon?"

"Oh, that actually has to do with his brothers," Clint told her. "Apparently, they want to meet me. I think maybe they don't really believe that he knows me."

"Well, maybe meeting you will impress them," she said, "and put them on the right path."

"I can't really say I've been traveling the right path, Gloria," he said. "It's sort of the path I got stuck with."

"I'm just saying," she went on, "maybe you can make sure they don't grow into outlaws."

"Well, I'll do my best, then," he said. He looked around. "You have some beautiful things here."

"Oh, go on," she said. "Now that you walked Nathan over here you can leave. You don't have to pretend to be impressed."

"But I am impressed."

"Thank you, but you certainly don't have to spend any more time in here than you need to."

"All right," he said, "but agree to have supper with me again tonight and I'll meet you here after closing."

"Very well," she said, "I agree."

"Four then?"

"Five," she said. "I told you many of the businesses close at four, but I close at five."

"All right, then," Clint said. "I'll see you at five."

She watched him as he left, and after the door closed she put both hands to her chest, where her heart was beating like a school girl's.

*****

In the back room Julia gave Nathan some errands to run and allowed the boy to go out the back door. Then she sat down and made the same motion, but both hands to her chest. Not only was her heart beating fast, but she could barely catch her breath.

Of course she knew who the Gunsmith was, but she didn't want to let her little brother see how meeting Clint Adams had affected her. He was much older than her, but suddenly her body was tingling and she was feeling funny. Julia was not a virgin, but that was only by virtue of some fumbling boys in a hayloft or two. She'd never been with a real man, and Clint Adams was certainly a real man.

She wondered, though, if Gloria Knight had already staked a claim to the man. If there was something going on there she certainly didn't want to come between them. Gloria was pretty enough, but she was very old, and Julia...well, Julia knew how pretty she was. Men and boys not only looked at her, but told her all the time. And she was so much younger than Gloria, why would a man not prefer her...

And in that moment she felt ashamed. She was having feeling unfamiliar to her. She had just meant Clint Adams, but thinking of him and Gloria night together was making her feel...jealousy?

That was crazy.

Wasn't it?

SEVENTEEN

"We ain't got a gun," Sam said, "how we gonna kidnap him? All we got's that hunting rifle that's only good for shootin' rabbit. It wouldn't even hurt a man."

"We got a gun," Ed said.

"Where?"

Ed went to the corner of their house, knelt down, and pried loose a floorboard. He took something from underneath the floor and put the board back, then carried it to the kitchen table. It was wrapped in a rag. He unwrapped it and left it on the table for his brother to see.

"Where'd you get a gun?" Sam asked, staring at the revolver.

"I found it."

"Where?"

Ed turned to face his brother and turned very serious. "You gotta promise you won't tell nobody."

"Who'm I gonna tell?"

"Just promise."

"I promise."

"Okay," Ed said. "I found a dead man, and he was wearing this gun."

"A dead man! Where?"

"About five miles south of here, when I was hunting. He was just lyin' there."

"Was he shot?"

"Naw," Ed said, "it looked like he got throwed from his horse and broke his neck."

"Was his horse there?"

"No, it must've run off, or I woulda gone through his saddlebags and brought the horse back here. We coulda used it."

Sam narrowed his eyes at his brother.

"Didja go through his pockets? Did he have any money? Yer supposed ta share—"

"He didn't have any money, Sam," Ed said, cutting his brother off. "All I got from him was this gun."

"What about the gun belt?"

"It snapped when he hit the ground. It was kinda worn, anyway."

"Julia woulda mended it—"

"I don't want no mended gun belt!" Ed snapped. "Look, stop askin' questions. You said we needed a gun, and we got one."

"Is it loaded?"

"Of course it's loaded."

"Did you shoot it?"

"Just once, to make sure it fired."

The two boys stood there and stared at the gun. By keeping it under the floorboards that way the dampness had already begun to affect the workings of the gun, but they didn't know that.

"Okay," Sam said, "so one of us is gonna have a gun, but we ain't gonna shoot 'im."

"No," Ed said. "We're gonna hit him over the head."

"With what?"

"We're gonna go out and find ourselves a good sized tree limb that we can use as a club, Then, when he ain't lookin', yer gonna hit him with it."

"Me? Why me?"

"Because I'm gonna have the gun."

"Why do you get to carry the gun?"

"Because I'm the oldest," Ed said, "and I'm the one who found it."

"Well...what if I hit him too hard and kill 'im?" Sam asked.

"You ain't gonna hit him too hard," Ed said. "Yer just gonna tap him, is all."

"How hard's a tap?"

"We got time to find the club and practice before noon." Ed grabbed the gun from the table and stuck it in his belt. "So, come on!"

*****

When Nathan got back to the house—he'd finished running the errands Julia had set for him—he found his brothers out back. Sam was swinging a tree limb while Ed watched. As he approached the two older boys saw him, And Sam pulled his shirt out over the gun he had tucked in his belt. He did not want to have to explain the gun to his little brother.

"There he is!" Ed called out. "How ya doin', Nathan?"

"I'm good," the boy said. "I did all Julia's work and she gave me four bits."

"Hand it over," Sam said.

Nathan handed the money to his older brother obediently. Ed then gave him a nickel, which he tucked away in his pocket.

"There you go," Ed said. "All even."

"Did you talk to the Gunsmith?" Sam asked.

"I sure did," Nathan said. "He's gonna meet us at noon."

"Behind the livery?" Ed asked.

"Just like you said."

"Attaboy!" Ed said, slapping Nathan on the back.

Nathan puffed out his chest and said, "You didn't think I could do it, did ya?"

"I knew you could do it," Ed said. "It was Sam here didn't think so." Ed looked at Sam. "See, what'd I tell ya? Nathan came through for us."

"He sure did," Sam said, a little sourly since he was taking the blame for something he didn't do.

"Whatcha doin' with that tree limb?" Nathan asked,

"Ah, nothin'," Sam said. "We was just messin' around until you got back."

"Let's go inside and have some lemonade," Ed said. "Julia made a pitcher."

"She said that was for dinner," Nathan warned.

"Come on," Ed said, nudging Nathan. "She won't care. Let's be brave."

"Okay," Nathan said, and ran for the house.

"What should I do with this?" Sam whispered, about the branch.

"Leave it out by the door," Ed said. "He won't notice it there."

"And the gun?"

"I have it," Ed said. "He won't see it."

"If he does—"

"If he does," Ed said, "we'll let him shoot it, and he'll keep his mouth shut. Now, come on."

The two brothers followed Nathan to the house.

EIGHTEEN

Greg Colter came out of the Purple Garter, squinting at the sunlight. He knew his brothers would be having breakfast down the street, at a café near their hotel. He'd spent a pleasant night and morning with the whore they bought him, but he was back to thinking about Clint Adams. If he saw him on the street right now he knew he'd brace him and draw on him and explain it to his brothers later.

But that didn't happen.

He walked down the street toward their hotel, which was the cheapest in town. It didn't even have a name, just a sign over the door that said HOTEL. And next to it was a small restaurant with a sign that said CAFÉ.

He walked in the door of the café, saw his brothers sitting at a table, filling their plates with large mounds of scrambled eggs and ham from platters in the center of the table. There was also a third plate there, waiting for him. Ken said he loved eating "family style," the way his mother used to do it, all; the food on the table at one time.

"Greg," Ken called out. "Come on over, brother. Dig right in."

Greg sat down, grabbed a fork, and started filling his plate.

"How was the girl?" Jerry asked, slapping his brother on the back.

"She was fine," Greg said.

"Come on," Ken said. "We know how you like redheads. That was one fine filly."

"I know what you're tryin' ta do" Greg said.

"What's that?" Ken asked.

"Tryin' ta distract me with a whore, and with food," Greg said. "Well, it ain't gonna work. I'm gonna kill the Gunsmith, fair and square."

"Fine with me," Ken said, "but not on the street. Understand?"

"Yeah, I understand. So," Greg asked, with a mouthful of eggs and ham, "when?"

"We'll talk about that later, little brother," Ken said. He looked at Jerry. "What about that money those two Tanner kids owe us?"

"Who, the Tanner brothers?" Jerry asked. "That's pennies, Ken."

"It ain't the money," Ken said. "It's the principle."

"The what?" Jerry asked.

"We can't let anybody think they can owe us money and get away with it."

"Well then," Jerry said, "I guess we oughtta go and find them."

"Or," Ken said, "that pretty big sister of theirs."

"You think she has the money to pay us?"

"She has a job, ain't she?" Ken asked. "And if not her, then that lady she works for should have it."

"Why would she pay their debt?" Jerry asked.

"Maybe," Ken said, "because she doesn't want that nice little dress shop to burn down."

Greg stopped eating.

"Fire?" he said.

If he liked anything more than his guns it was setting something on fire.

"Yes, Greg," Ken said, putting his arm around his little brother's shoulders, "fire. How would you like to set a store on fire?"

"And watch it burn?"

"Oh yeah," Ken said, "we can watch it burn."

"When?" Finally, Ken thought, something else got his mind off the Gunsmith.

"Finish your breakfast," Ken said, "and we'll see about it."

NINETEEN

Clint spent the rest of the morning sitting in a chair in front of his hotel, watching the town go by. When it was nearing 11:30 he stood up and started for the livery to keep his promise to Nathan. First he wanted to stop in and check up on Eclipse.

As he entered he saw the man everybody called Hoss working on another horse's hoof. When he saw Clint he dropped it and stood straight.

"Checkin' on your animal?"

"That's right."

"He's right back here," Hoss said. "I took care of the shoes."

He took Clint to a stall where Eclipse stood. The Darley Arabian's coat looked as if it was glowing. He entered the stall and ran his hand over the horse's back.

"He looks good," Clint said.

"I'm takin' good care of him."

"I guess you figure if the sheriff arrests me and locks me up, you'll be able to keep him, huh?"

"W-what?" the man stammered. "I don't know what you mean."

Clint came out of the stall and faced Hoss, looked up at him.

"Somebody told the sheriff I was in town," he said. "Do you know who that was?"

"Y-you don't think it was me, do ya?" Hoss asked.

"It was either you, or the clerk at my hotel," Clint said.

"Which clerk?"

"I don't know," Clint said. "The one who checked me in was young, polite—wait, that doesn't help. Everybody in this town is polite. He was a skinny fella in his thirties—"

"That's Benny," Hoss said. "He probably did it."

"Why do you say that?"

"There are three hotels in town," Hoss said, "and each one has a clerk that tells the sheriff when a stranger gets to town."

"Okay," Clint said, "that's kinda what I figured."

"So, you really didn't think I did it?"

"No," Clint said, "but I needed you to confirm what I thought about the town's hotels."

Hoss seemed to heave a great sigh of relief.

"He looks good," Clint said, running his hand over Eclipse's rump. "Thanks for taking good care of him."

"Oh, yes sir," Hoss said. "It's my pleasure. Will you, uh, be needin' him today?"

"No," Clint said.

"Tomorrow?"

"Maybe," Clint said. "I'll let you know, Hoss."

"Okay."

As Clint left, Hoss went back to working on the other horse.

Clint left the livery by the front entrance, then circled around to meet young Nathan and his brothers in the back.

*****

The three Tanner brothers—Ed, Sam, and Nathan—got to the livery before Clint Adams, and took up position behind it.

"He should be here any minute," Nathan said, anxiously.

Ed had taken Nathan by the shoulder and walked with him ahead of Sam, who took up the rear, carrying his tree branch club behind his back. Ed had told him that the minute Clint Adams wasn't looking at him he was to swing the club and hit him in the head.

"When he's knocked out," Ed said, "I'll grab his gun belt and then we'll tie him up."

Sam was still hoping he didn't hit the man too hard and accidently kill him. They wouldn't get any money for a dead man.

"Nathan," Ed said, "when your friend gets here you take the lead and make the introductions. After all, he's your friend, right?"

"That's right," Nathan said. "Okay, Ed. I'll do it."

"Good boy."

Ed didn't like how nervous Sam was looking, so as Nathan kept an eye out for Clint Adams, he went over to stand next to his other brother.

"Calm down," he said.

"I'm nervous."

"You're gonna give us away," Ed said. "We don't want Nathan to know somethin's up, and we sure don't want Clint Adams to know. You'll get us both killed."

"Killed?"

"Nobody's gettin' killed," Ed said, sorry he'd mentioned the word. "Just do like I say and relax. When Nathan introduces us I'll move around so that Adams has to face me, and put his back to you. That's when you let him have it."

"Okay, Ed."

Ed moved back over to where Nathan was standing

Sam could feel his hands sweating, and he hoped he wouldn't drop the tree limb.

Suddenly, a man appeared from the side of the barn and Nathan yelled, "Hey, Clint."

Sam didn't drop the club.

But he almost crapped his pants.

TWENTY

Clint saw Nathan standing with two other boys and waving excitedly. As he approached them he noticed the resemblance.

Nathan smiled broadly and turned to speak to one of the boys, who looked like the older brother of the three. The other brother looked nervous at the prospect of meeting Clint.

"Hello, Nathan," Clint said as he reached the boys.

"Hi, Clint," Nathan said. "This is my brother Ed, and that's my brother Sam."

"Hello, fellas," Clint said.

"Mr. Adams," Ed said, extending his hand. "It's a pleasure."

Clint shook hands with Ed, then looked at Sam, who seemed to be holding back.

"Don't mind him," Ed said. "He's nervous."

"No reason to be nervous," Clint said.

"That's what I keep tellin' him," Ed said, moving a bit to stand near Nathan. To face them, Clint had to turn slightly, putting Sam just a little behind him. Later he realized how careless he'd been because they were kids—well, because Nathan was a kid, and he was so excited. When the branch came crashing down on his head, the lights went out, and he crumpled to the ground...

*****

"Is he dead?" Sam asked, anxiously.

"Naw, he ain't dead," Ed said leaning over Clint.

Nathan was just staring, and finally he yelled, "What did you do that for?"

"Take it easy, Nathan," Ed said.

""He's my friend," Nathan went on. "Why'd you do that?"

"We had to," Ed said. "Kid, we gotta make some money, and this is the best way."

"Hittin' him over the head?" Nathan asked.

"Kidnappin' him," Sam said. "We're kidnappin' the Gunsmith."

"That's crazy!" Nathan said. "Julia ain't gonna like this at all!"

"Now Nathan," Ed said, taking hold of Nathan by the shoulder, "you can't tell Julia anythin'. Look, we're doin' this for the family. As soon as we get paid we'll let him go."

"Get paid how much?" Nathan asked.

"Don't worry, little man," Ed said, "you'll get your cut."

"I ain't worried about that," Nathan said. He looked down at Clint. "Are you sure he ain't dead?"

Ed leaned over Clint, whose hat had been knocked askew, but was still on. He took it off and checked his scalp.

"Ah, he ain't even cut," Ed said. "You did good, Sam."

Sam tossed away the branch he was holding while Ed unstrapped Clint's gun belt. He stood up and strapped it on his own waist.

"Hey!" Sam said. "Now you got two guns."

"You got a gun?" Nathan asked.

Ed lifted his shirt, took the gun from his belt, and handed it to Sam, who accepted it eagerly.

"Now you got a gun," Ed said. "Okay, now we gotta move him."

"Don't you think we better tie him up?" Sam asked.

"That's a good idea," Ed said. "I'm surprised you came up with it. Find some rope. We gotta move him before somebody comes back here."

Ed looked around. He hadn't thought of this before. They needed a horse, or a buckboard, to move Clint Adams, and move him...where?

"Looks what I found," Sam said.

Ed turned and saw Sam standing there with a wheel-barrow.

"Jesus, Sam," Ed said, "you keep comin' up with good idea today. Help me get him in."

They lifted Clint's inert body and put him in the wheelbarrow, then used a rope Sam had found to bind his arms behind him, and his ankles.

"Okay," Ed said, "let's go."

"Where?" Nathan asked. "Where are you takin' him?"

"I think I have a place," Ed said. "Come on."

"I gotta go—" Nathan started, but Ed grabbed him by the shirt and yanked him back.

"Sorry, little man," Ed said, "but you're comin' with us. You're part of this."

"I ain't so!"

"Yeah, you are," Ed said. "You're the one that got him here. Julia would be real mad, and the sheriff would arrest you right along with us."

"Arrest?" Sam said.

Ed looked at him. "Nobody's getting' arrested." Then looked back at Nathan. "But if we do get arrested, we all get arrested."

'That ain't fair!" Nathan complained.

"No, it ain't," Ed said, "so you better work with us and make sure we don't get locked up. Now come on!"

Nathan looked at his new friend, Clint Adams, all trussed up in the wheelbarrow and—heart sinking—followed his brothers.

TWENTY-ONE

When Clint woke with a headache it was dark. He tried to move, but realized he was tied hand and foot. He looked around, saw some light coming from in between some boards, and realized he was in some kind of shack.

He settled back to take stock. Obviously, somebody had hit him over the head. It had to be the other brother, Sam. He'd been foolish enough to turn his back on the boy. But that was because of Nathan. He didn't know if the younger brother had any idea what the other two were up to—in fact, he had no idea what they were up to. What was the point of taking him captive?

At that moment he heard the door being unlocked, and then the interior of the shack was flooded with light.

The light blinded him, but after a moment he knew it was Ed, and he could see that he was wearing his gun belt.

"What the hell do you think you're doing?" Clint asked.

"Right now I'm just checkin' to see how you are," Ed told him.

"I've got a headache," Clint said, "and I'm mad. If you know what's good for you, you'll untie me right now."

"I can't do that, Mr. Adams," Ed said. "Not for a while, yet. Just be patient and later I'll bring you something to eat."

"You and your brothers are going to be in a lot of trouble."

"I don't think we have to bring the law into this."

"I'm not talking about the law, son,' Clint said. "You're in trouble with me."

"Now take it easy, Mr. Adams," Ed said. "We don't mean you no harm. We're just gonna keep ya here a little while, is all. And don't go blaming Nathan. My little brother didn't know nothin' about this. It was all my idea."

"But," Clint said, "you're not the one who hit me from behind, are you?"

"I can see yer mad," Ed said. "I'll bring you some food later, and maybe you'll calm down."

"Hey, wait—" Clint said, but Ed backed out and closed the door, and Clint heard a padlock being set.

He sat back and considered his options.

*****

"How is he?" Sam asked.

The three brothers were in an old line shack that had been abandoned many years ago. Clint had been locked in an old tool shed nearby, also abandoned.

"He's got a headache and he's sort of mad," Ed said.

"How mad?" Sam asked.

"Pretty mad."

"He oughtta be," Nathan said. "He's gonna be mad at me, too, ain't he?"

"I told him you had nothin' to do with it," Ed said.

"But he's gonna be mad at me," Sam said. "I'm the one who hit him."

"Look, we're gonna let him go," Ed said, "as soon as we collect the ransom."

"What ransom?" Nathan asked.

"What?" Ed asked.

"I said what ransom?"

Ed and Sam exchanged a look.

*****

Clint stretched out his legs, which had started to cramp. He was tied at the ankles and the wrists. From the way the walls looked, a good kick might have taken one down. But if he did that he'd still be tied hand and foot, and the noise would alert his captors. He needed to get his hands and feet free first before he tried to get out of the shack.

He looked around for something that might cut the ropes on his wrists. It was fairly obvious he was in an old abandoned tool shed, but unfortunately, it had not been abandoned with tools in it. If only there was one tool, even if it was rusted with age.

He shifted position because his butt had started to fall asleep, but also to see if there was anything behind him.

Nothing.

They said they were going to feed him. Maybe they'd free his hands for that, and he'd have a chance to make a move then.

So all there was for him to do at the moment was wait.

*****

"That shows how young you are, Nathan," Ed said, "and why I do the thinkin'. There's always a ransom when there's a kidnappin'."

"Yeah, but," Nathan said, "who's gonna pay the ransom?"

Ed looked at Sam, who looked right back with his eyebrows raised.

"Okay, Ed," he said, "you're the one who does the thinkin', right?"

"That's right."

"Well, little brother's got a good question," Sam said, pointing at Nathan. "Who's gonna pay a ransom for the Gunsmith?"

Ed stared at Sam and Nathan and scratched his head.

He hadn't thought of that.

TWENTY-TWO

"Anything else you want me to do before I go, Gloria?" Julia asked.

"No, Julia," Gloria said from behind the counter. "We're done for the day. Tomorrow you can start separating those buttons. I know it's a tedious job but—"

"It's all right," Julia said with a smile. "Somebody's got to do it."

"Thank you, Julia," Gloria said. "What are your plans for tonight?"

"Nothing," Julia said. "I have to go home and make supper for the boys."

"Can't you let them fend for themselves?" Gloria asked. "Two of them are old enough."

"Yes, but not Nathan."

"Why don't you and Nathan have supper with me?" Gloria asked. "I'll take you both out. We'll have steaks."

"Aren't you—isn't Mr. Adams coming—"

"He was supposed to," Gloria said. She checked her watch. "He's late. Maybe he's not coming."

"I appreciate the offer, but I can't," Julia said. "The boys, they really can't, you know."

"Can't what?"

"Take care of themselves."

"So you're their sister and their mother?"

"I'm afraid so."

"You need to find yourself a young man, Julia," Gloria said. "Maybe if you got married, your brothers would have to learn to care for themselves."

"Not Nathan," Julia said. "Ed and Sam couldn't take care of Nathan."

"Well then, you could take him with you," Gloria said. "Look, I'm sorry. I'm holding you up. I'll wait a little longer, see if Mr. Adams puts in an appearance. Maybe he just...lost interest."

"He doesn't seem like that kind of man to me," Julia said. "Besides, you're much too pretty. A man wouldn't lose interest in you."

"That's very sweet of you, Julia," Gloria said, "but look in a mirror some time. I mean, really look."

Julia frowned. "Why?"

Gloria smiled. Could a girl who was this beautiful really not know?

"Just look some time," Gloria said. "You'll see."

"Goodnight," Julia said, a bit confused.

"Goodnight."

*****

Julia hurried home to prepare supper and found that none of her brothers were home. Something was going on with them—at least, with Ed and Sam. And if they were dragging Nathan into it, she was going to have both their asses.

She filled the stove with wood and started supper...

*****

After Julia left the store Gloria walked to the door and locked it. She peered out the window, and there was no sign of Clint Adams. Julia said he didn't strike her as the kind of man to lose interest. He didn't strike Gloria that way, either, but maybe he got a better offer, maybe at the Purple Garter.

Gloria knew that her age did not work in her favor when it came to attracting men. Certainly having Julia in the store with her brought that home every day. Not many men came into the store, but when they—with their wives, or sisters, or whoever—they usually could not keep their eyes off Julia. Even in that way Clint seemed different. Of course, he admired her, but he didn't seem as fixated on her as most men were.

She looked out the window again, then sighed and walked back into the store. She had some work that would keep her there for about another half an hour. Maybe he'd show up by then, with a valid excuse for being late...He was just going to have to explain it to her when she left her shop.

*****

Oddly, being all trussed up like he was, Clint still thought about Gloria Knight. He was supposed to have supper with her, and she'd be waiting for him. He hoped she wouldn't think that he stayed away by choice, but why wouldn't she?

He wondered when Nathan's brother Ed was going to return with that food he promised?

*****

When the door opened and her three brothers walked in Julia turned from the stove and looked at them.

"Where have you boys been?" she demanded.

"Out," Ed said, "but we're back now and we're hungry." Ed slapped Nathan on the back. "Go and get washed up for supper, little man."

Just the fact that Ed told Nathan that proved that something was going on. She knew they'd never tell her straight out, so she was going to have to find out for herself.

"All of you get washed," she said. "Supper in ten minutes."

TWENTY-THREE

Ed knew he was going to have to figure out a way to get some food to Clint Adams after supper. Julia had made chicken, so he managed to secret a couple of pieces in his pockets while seated at the table.

Julia cleared the leftovers from the table and noticed that the boys had been particularly hungry. There was more chicken gone than usual. Of course, Nathan might have found himself another animal, and was hiding food to take to it again. But chicken? What kind of animal ate chicken?

*****

After supper Ed pulled Sam aside and said, "Here, take this to Adams." He handed him a napkin with chicken wrapped in it.

"Me? Why me?"

"Because if I go Julia will notice," Ed said. "And I've got to keep Nathan here."

"Are you thinkin' Nathan might let him go?"

"I just want to make sure," Ed said. "Now go. And get back quick."

"Ed, should I untie him so he can eat?"

"If you untie him he'll be on you in a minute," Ed said. "So what am I supposed to do? Feed him?"

"Exactly," Ed said. "Feed him. I put some potatoes in there, too."

*****

Clint heard someone approaching and then the door to the shack opened. It was dusk so there was no light to blind him. He recognized Sam, the middle brother.

"I brung you some food," the boy said.

"Are you going to untie my hands so I can eat it?"

"No," Sam said, hunkering down, "Ed said I got to feed it to you."

"You always do what Ed tells you to do?"

"He's my older brother," Sam said. "He does the thinking. Here."

Sam held a chicken leg out to Clint, and he took a bite.

"That's very good," Clint said. "Julia make that?"

"Yeah," Sam said. "Julia's a real good cook. Try a potato." He popped one into Clint's mouth. "Sorry about my fingers."

"That's all right," Clint said. "So, if Ed does the thinking, kidnapping me was his idea."

"Well, yeah."

"And by now you realize what a mistake you made."

"What mistake?" Sam asked, looking worried.

"More chicken, please?"

Sam held the leg out and Clint took another bite.

"I mean," Clint said, "there's nobody to demand a ransom from. Nobody will pay for me."

"Ed's thinkin' about that," Sam said. "He'll think of somethin'."

"No, he won't," Clint said. "There's nobody he can think of. Nobody. Potato?"

Sam popped another in, harder this time. Clint almost choked.

"Sorry," Sam said, sheepishly. "Just eat, okay? Stop talkin'. I gotta get back."

"Okay, Sam," Clint said. "I'll stop talking." He actually wanted to make sure he got to eat all the food the boy brought. He had to keep his strength up, since he had no idea how long he'd be there.

*****

Sam was on his way back to the house as it was getting dark, and suddenly there were two men blocking his way.

"Hey, Sammy," Ken Colter said. "How you doin'?"

Sam turned to go in the other direction, but was blocked by Greg Colter.

"Now, take it easy, Sammy," Ken said, standing shoulder to shoulder with Jerry. "We just wanna talk to you."

"About what?" Sam asked.

"About money," Jimmy said.

"Look," Sam said, "I know we owe you money. My brother Ed is workin' on somethin'—"

"Like what?" Ken asked.

"I—I can't tell you that."

"Why not?"

"I—I just can't."

"Well, maybe Ed can tell us," Ken said. "Why don't you tell him to come and see us?"

"I—s-sure, sure, I'll tell him."

"Yeah, you will," Ken said, "but we'll just send him a little message with you."

"M-message?" Sam asked. "W-what kind of message?"

"The kind you won't have to remember to deliver," Ken said. He nodded to his brothers.

"Wha—" Sam started, but Greg stepped in from behind and punched him in the kidney. Sam went down to the ground, and didn't remember anything after that.

TWENTY-FOUR

Ed was waiting out in front of the house for Sam to get back. Julia had already made Nathan go to bed. When he saw his brother coming he knew something was wrong. Sam couldn't seem to stay on his feet. He ran out to meet him.

"Sam," Ed said, grabbing his brother before he could fall. "What happened?"

"The Colters," Sam said. "T-they caught me as I was comin' back. Said—said they was sending you a message."

"Ah, Sam," Ed said. "Come on, let's get you inside."

"But—but Julia—"

"Julia knows that the Colters are crazy," Ed said, helping his brother to his feet, "just don't say anythin' about the Gunsmith."

"Yeah, yeah, I know..."

Ed helped Sam walk to the house and as they went inside Julia saw them.

"Sam! What happened?" she yelled.

"He ran into the Colters."

"Those animals!" She turned on Ed. "Do you still owe them money?"

"Well...maybe."

"Didn't I tell you—"

"Julia," Ed said, "we gotta get Sam into a chair."

"Yes, all right," Julia said. "Get him to a chair. I'll get some water."

Ed half carried half dragged Sam to a chair and sat him down.

"Anythin' broke?" Ed asked.

"I don't think so," Sam said. "I just...hurt."

"Move, Ed!" Julia ordered.

Ed stepped aside and Julia knelt in front of Sam and started cleaning his wounds. He had a gash on his head and was bleeding from a cut lip.

"You need a doctor," she said. "Ed?"

"I can go and get him," Ed said. "I'll be right back."

As Ed went out the front door Nathan came out of his room.

"What happened?"

"Go back to bed, Nathan."

"No," he said. "I wanna know what happened."

"Some men beat up Sam, Nathan," Julia said. "Get me some more cloths."

"All right."

"Julia," Sam said.

"What?"

"You shouldn't have let Ed go alone."

"Ed will be fine," she said. "He knows how not to be seen."

"The Colters..."

"How much money do you and Ed owe the Colters, Sam?" Julia asked.

"I-I don't know," Sam said. "Only Ed knows."

"And why do you owe them money?"

"We lost...at poker," Sam said.

"Oh Sam," Julia said, "I told you and Ed not to gamble."

"I know," Sam said. "I'm sorry."

Nathan brought Julia some more cloths. She soaked them and cleaned Sam's face.

"Where else does it hurt?"

"My ribs..."

She opened his shirt, saw that he was already starting to bruise.

"You might have some cracked ribs. What did they do?"

"They kicked me while I was down."

"Cowards!"

"I'll be all right."

"Just sit still, Sam," she said. "The doctor will be here soon."

"I'll go outside and watch for them," Nathan said.

*****

When Ed left the house he ran for town. Briefly, he considered retrieving Clint Adams' gun, but he couldn't do that without Julia seeing. He also thought about releasing the Gunsmith, but there was no guarantee the man would help. Besides, he had come up with another idea.

If he couldn't figure out somebody who would pay a ransom for the Gunsmith, maybe he'd be able to find somebody who might want to buy him. Like maybe the Colters. Or maybe they'd take him in exchange for the money he and Sam owed them.

He got to town and ran to the doctor's office. The doc answered after he pounded on it for a few minutes.

"What the hell are you pounding on my door for? Who is that?"

"It's Ed Tanner, Doc."

"Whatta ya want?"

"My, uh, my sister, Julia, sent me for you."

"Your sister?" the doctor said. He was an older man with white hair, and Ed knew he had a soft spot for Julia. "She's a sweet girl. What's wrong with her?"

"She wants you to come to our house real quick," Ed told him. "It's an emergency."

"All right, all right," the man said. "Let me get my bag."

While he waited Ed hoped the sawbones would still treat Sam when he found out it wasn't Julia who needed some fixing.

TWENTY-FIVE

Waiting to be fed hadn't helped. Clint still didn't have a way to get out of his predicament, but at least he wasn't hungry anymore.

It was pitch black outside, and even darker inside. If the brothers had gone home to the house they shared with their sister Julia, he could kick his way out of the shack. But what then? Hop away? And what if one of them—Ed? Sam?—was still around, just in case he did escape?

He decided to wait until morning. If all they wanted to do was collect a ransom, he didn't think there was any plan that involved killing him. He found a relatively comfortable position, and went to sleep.

*****

The Colters were once again sitting in the Purple Garter, but instead of fighting and breaking chairs, they were just talking.

"Where do you suppose that kid was comin' from?" Ken asked.

"Who knows?" Jerry asked. "As long as he took the message back to his big brother."

"When do I get a chance at the Gunsmith?" Greg asked impatiently.

"Relax, Greg," Ken said. "There's plenty of time for that."

Greg looked over at the next table, where three of their gang members were drinking and back-slapping.

"Go and join them and have a good time," Ken told his younger brother. "Let me and Jerry talk."

"Talk, talk," Greg said, "that's all you ever wanna do." He finished his drink, then stood up. "Yeah, I will go and have a good time. Let me know what you decide after all your talkin'."

As Greg walked away, Jerry asked, "You ain't really gonna let him make a try for the Gunsmith, are you?"

"Have you seen the Gunsmith today?"

"No."

"So maybe we don't have to worry," Ken said. "Maybe he ain't even in town, anymore."

"But what if he is?"

"Then if Greg wants to try him, we'll let him," Ken said. "We'll just be right there to back his play."

Jerry poured himself another drink from the half finished bottle on the table.

*****

The doctor patched Sam up and told Julia that he'd be fine after a good night's sleep. Then he tossed Ed an annoyed lock and left.

"Why's he so mad?" Nathan asked.

"Yes," Julia said, "what about that? What did you tell him?"

"I may have let him think you were the one hurt, just to get him here," Ed said.

"Well," Julia said, "you got him here, that's all that counts. Let's get Sam into his bed."

Between them Julia and Ed got Sam to his bed, where he immediately fell asleep. Then they went out and sat at the kitchen table.

"Nathan," Julia said, "go to bed."

"Aw Julia..."

"Go!"

Nathan started for the room he shared with his brothers, but turned back before he made it to the door.

"Ed, you gonna tell 'er about Clint?"

"Nathan!" Ed snapped. "Go to bed!"

"What did he mean?" Julia asked, as Nathan went to his room. "What about Clint?"

"Nothin'," Ed said. "We just met 'im, is all."

"You're up to somethin', Ed," Julia said. "Don't think I don't know that. Does it have something to do with Mr. Adams?"

Ed didn't answer.

"He was supposed to have supper with Mrs. Knight," Julia said, "but he didn't show up. Do you know why?"

"Julia...don't worry..."

"Ed," she said, leaning forward, "what did you do?"

Ed stared back...

*****

"Whatta you wanna do?" Jerry asked.

"I'll tell you somethin'," Ken said to his brother, "I like those kids."

"Why?"

"They remind me of us when we wuz kids," Ken said. "They're always lookin' for a way to make money. That kid wasn't out tonight just takin' a walk. He was up to somethin', and it's somethin' they think they can make money on."

"So you wanna ask 'em?"

"I think," Ken said, "we should ask the older one, Ed. He's the brains."

"You mean, like you?" Jerry asked.

Ken grinned, took a drink ,and said, "Yeah, I mean exactly like me."

TWENTY-SIX

"You what?" Julia screeched.

"Now, don't get all upset."

"You tell me that you kidnapped the Gunsmith—hit him over the head—and you don't want me to get upset?"

The one thing Julia had inherited from their mother—other than her cooking talent—was her temper. It was why Sam and Nathan were afraid of her. It was why Ed was always careful around her.

"Look," Ed said, "we owe the Colters money. You see what they did to Sam, and that was just a message. Now I don't mean your precious Gunsmith any harm. I just want to ransom him so we can get enough money to pay off the Colters, and still have some left for us."

"You have to let him go!"

"And we will," Ed said, "As soon as we get some money."

Julia took a deep breath and said in a low, controlled, angry tone, "Ed, where is he?"

Ed sat back and folded his arms. "I ain't gonna tell you."

She half rose from her chair and said, "Yes, you are."

"You scare Nathan and Sam, Julia," Ed said, "but you don't scare me. I'm the oldest male. It's my job to take care of us."

"Your job?" Julia repeated with a laugh. "Then you've been doin' a piss poor job of it. You don't even have a job!"

"I ain't gonna need one," Ed said, "after we get paid for the Gunsmith."

"Paid by who?" she demanded. "Who's gonna pay a ransom for him? Does he have family?"

"I don't know."

"Do you know who his friends are?"

"Not exactly."

"What do you know about him?"

"Just, you know, what I heard..."

"This is typical of your thinking, Ed," she said. "You didn't think this through, at all."

"Then help me," Ed said. "You're smart. Whatta you think we should do with him?"

"Let him go!"

Ed thought for a minute.

"You think he'd pay us to let him go?"

"No!" she shouted. "Just let him go!"

"I can't do that," Ed said. "He's too valuable."

"To who?"

"I got another idea."

"And what's that?"

"We could sell 'im."

"To who?"

Ed shrugged, and said, "I don't know yet. Help me figure it out." He leaned forward. "Julia, this is a chance for our family. Don't you want Nathan to have a good life?"

"Of course."

"You don't want him to turn out like me, do you?"

She hesitated, then her face softened. "Oh, Ed, you ain't so bad, really—"

"I'm on a bad path, Julia," he admitted, "and I'm takin' Sam with me. I don't wanna take Nathan, too."

She sat back in her chair and stared at her brother.

"Look, Julia," he said, "stop yellin' at me and just take tonight to think about it. Adams ain't hurt, and he's in a safe place. Just think about it."

"All right, Ed," she agreed, because she was tired, "I'll think about it."

"Good," he said, "that's all I ask."

He stood up.

"Where are you going?" she asked.

"I'm just gonna sit out on the porch," he said, "you know, the way Papa usedta. To think."

She stood up too, walked over to him, and kissed him on the cheek.

"I do love you, Ed."

"I love you, too, Julia," he said. "That's why I'm doin' this."

"I'm gonna check on Sam."

He nodded, and went outside. Once he was there with the door closed he rolled himself a cigarette and sat down to smoke it.

*****

Julia checked on Sam, who seemed to be sleeping comfortably, then crossed the room to look at Nathan, also asleep.

She left the room and went back to sit at the kitchen table. Ed wanted her to think about it, and by agreeing to do that she surprised herself. Maybe Ed was right, maybe this was the only way they were ever going to make money as a family. She did want a better life for Nathan, maybe enough money to send him away to school. Would the Gunsmith begrudge them that? After all, he wasn't hurt.

Finding someone who would pay a ransom would keep him that way. But selling him...who would want to buy him except some enemy, who would then want to kill him? Could she live with herself if that happened?

TWENTY-SEVEN

The light came into the shack through the space between the boards that made up the walls. He was still convinced he could kick through them, but not yet.

Somebody was bound to come with some food for him for breakfast. Maybe he could convince them—after everybody had a night's sleep—to release him.

His stomach rumbled, and he wondered what Julia would be making for breakfast.

*****

"Are you gonna bring him some food?" Julia asked Ed at the table.

"Well, sure," he said. "That's what Sam was doin' last night when the Colters grabbed him."

"Is that where that extra chicken went?"

"Yeah."

"Can I go?" Nathan asked, looking up from his flapjacks. Sam was still in bed.

"No," Ed said.

"Why not?"

"You gotta stay here with Sam," Ed said. "He might need somethin'."

"Julia can do that!" Nathan argued.

"Julia has to go to work," Ed said. "You stay here. Now eat your breakfast."

"I'll make some bacon," Julia said. "You can take him that."

"Okay," Ed said.

"Can we have some bacon?" Nathan asked.

Julia smiled and said, "Sure."

*****

Julia left for work before Ed left to bring Clint his food, but she didn't really go. She went around to the side of the house, hid herself there, and waited for Ed to leave.

Then she followed him.

*****

Ed thought Julia seemed much calmer this morning about the whole situation. Maybe she had come around to his way of thinking.

He was so busy being on the lookout for the Colters that he didn't notice his sister following him.

*****

Julia trailed Ed to the old abandoned line shack, but was surprised when he didn't go in. Instead, he went behind the line shack to a small tool shed, used a key to unlock a padlock, then went inside.

*****

"My sister made you some bacon."

"Your sister? She knows I'm here?"

"No," Ed said, "but she knows we have you."

"Then she'll let me go."

"I wouldn't count on that," Ed said, "not even if she knew where you were."

"You're not wearing my gun."

"No," Ed said, "it's inside the house, and I didn't want Julia to know I have it."

"I see. And my hands?"

"I'll feed it to you."

"Fine."

Ed hunkered down and stuck a piece of bacon into Clint's mouth.

"Have you figured out yet who would ransom me?" he asked.

"No, not yet."

"You won't, you know," Clint said. "There's nobody who will pay a ransom for me."

"Then we'll have to go with my other idea," Ed said, giving Clint another piece of bacon.

"What's that?"

"I'll sell you."

"To who?"

"The highest bidder."

Clint didn't like the sound of that. While there was no one to ransom him, there was any number of people out there who would buy him just for the pleasure of killing him.

Of course, he knew he had friends who *would* pay a ransom for him—Bat Masterson, Talbot Roper, Rick Hartman—but he wasn't about to tell Ed Tanner that.

Ed gave him the last piece of bacon and then straightened up.

"Ed," he said, "this can only end badly."

"You don't know the half of it," Ed said. "My brother Sam already got beat up."

"Why?"

"We owe a lot of money to the Colter Gang," Ed said. "Grabbing you was gonna get us out from under that debt."

"The Colters."

"You heard of them?"

"Only since I got to town."

"Well, they'll kill us if we don't pay," Ed said. "And I don't know what they'll do to Julia and Nathan."

"Well," Clint said, "untie me and we'll make sure they don't do anything."

"I can't do that," Ed said.

"I'll help you and your family."

"After what we did?" Ed asked. "Hittin' you on the head, tyin' you up and all?"

"Why not?"

"I can't trust you."

Ed backed out the door and started to close it.

"Think it over, Ed," Clint called out. "I can get you out from under the debt."

"And then what? We're back where we started, with no money."

"But nobody will be trying to kill you."

"I'll think about it," Ed said, closing the door.

Clint listened to the padlock being closed again, and then heard Ed walking away.

The Tanner family was in trouble. That was a new piece of information, and one he might exploit.

He was starting to think he might be able to talk his way out of this.

TWENTY-EIGHT

Julia waited until Ed was out of sight, then walked to the tool shed. The padlock was closed, and she had no key. She looked around, but didn't see anything she could use to pry it open. Besides, she didn't think she was strong enough.

"Mr. Adams?" she called. "Can you hear me?"

*****

Clint listened while Ed's footsteps faded, then suddenly they were coming back—only they sounded different. Then he heard the voice.

"Mr. Adams? Can you hear me?"

"Who's that?" he called back. "Julia?"

"Yes, it's me," she said. "I'm so sorry about this. I just found out last night."

"Julia," he asked, "can you get me out of here?"

"I—I can't," she said. "I don't have a key, and I'm not strong enough to pry this lock open."

"Can you go and get help?"

"Help?" she repeated. "From who?"

He thought about saying "the sheriff," but decided against it. He didn't have too much confidence in the lawman.

"How about your boss? Mrs. Knight? If you tell her where I am she'll know what to do."

"I—I guess I could do that, but...if I do that my brothers will get into trouble."

"There won't be any trouble," he said. "Not from me. I promise."

"But they—they knocked you out. And kidnapped you."

"I just want to get out, Julia," he said. "Besides, your brothers have more trouble then me from the Colters."

"They—they owe them money."

"I know. How are they going to pay?"

"Ed says he can get money for you."

"Julia, if he sells me, it'll be to somebody who will kill me," Clint said. "Do you want that on your conscience?"

"N-No, of course not."

"Then get me out of here and I'll help."

"I—I'll have to think about it," she said. "I don't know what to do."

"Don't take too long," Clint said. "The Colters may not wait much longer for their money."

"I'm sorry," Julia said. "I have to go."

"Julia," Clint said, "you need my help."

"I'll come back," she said, "soon."

"Julia? Julia?"

But she was gone.

*****

Julia started to walk away from the tool shed, and then started running. She didn't stop running until she reached the outskirts of town, then she slowed to a walk. She wanted to catch her breath before she got to the store.

She could have gone right inside and told Gloria Knight what happened, and Mrs. Knight would do something to get Clint Adams out of that shed. But then what would happen to her family? Clint said there wouldn't be any trouble, but could she trust him? She didn't know him at all, only by reputation. According to his reputation, he'd probably kill her brothers. If not, he'd have them arrested. And would that include Nathan?

She didn't know what to do, so she just decided not to do anything for the moment. Go to work, then go home and make supper. By then maybe she would have thought of something, or maybe Ed would have come up with something.

When she entered the store Gloria looked at her from behind the counter.

"I'm sorry I'm late," she said. "My brother—"

"Your brothers again, yes, yes," Gloria said. "I was sure it was something like that. You don't have to make excuses for them, Julia."

"I'll—I'll just get to work on those buttons," she said.

TWENTY-NINE

Ed made a decision, and decided not to tell Sam or Julia about it.

"Nathan," he said, "keep an eye on Sam, take him anything he wants. But make sure he stays in bed."

"Where are you goin'?" Nathan asked.

"I have to go to town for a little while."

"What about Clint?" Nathan asked. "He's still in that shed."

"I'll take him some food from town," Ed said.

"Can't I take him some food?"

"Sure," Ed said, "tonight. You can take him his supper. How's that?"

"That's fine."

"I'll be back soon."

*****

Ed went right to town to look for the Colter Brothers. Actually, he wanted to find Ken Colter. Jerry was too stupid, and Greg was too quick to pull his gun. He'd just as soon shoot Ed as look at him. No, just like he was the smarter Tanner brother, it was Ken who was the smart Colter brother.

It was past breakfast time, so the place he'd most likely find Ken Colter was the Purple Garter.

"Whiskey?" the bartender asked Ken Colter.

"Coffee," Ken said.

The bartender brought him a cup of coffee.

"Where are your brothers?"

"I don't know," Ken said. "I think Jerry's still asleep. And Greg? Is he upstairs?"

"He might be."

"Shit," Ken said. "Look, bring me a pot. When I'm done with that, I'll have a whiskey. Got it, Big Bill?"

"Got it, Ken."

Big Bill turned to go back to the bar. It was too early for other customers, so it was only he and Ken Colter there for now. Except...

"Ken."

Colter looked at Big Bill, then at the door. Ed Tanner was standing just inside the batwings.

"Bring another cup, Bill."

"Right."

"You got my message," Ken said to Ed.

"I got it."

"Come on over here and have some coffee with me," Ken said. "Let's talk."

Ed walked stiffly to Ken Colter's table and sat across from him. Big Bill came over with another coffee cup. He set it down, then filled it and went back to the bar.

"How's your brother?"

"Busted up."

"Aw, he's not too bad," Ken said. "He walked home, didn't he?"

"You didn't have to do that."

"I needed to get your attention," Ken said. "And I did. Look, you're here. At least, I assume you came in here lookin' for me."

"I did."

"What's on your mind?"

"Our debt."

"Good, it's on my mind, too. What do you want to do about it?"

"I wanna pay it off."

"You got the money?"

"No."

"Then how do you propose to pay it off?"

"I got somethin' else."

"And what might that be?"

"I got the Gunsmith."

Ken sat back in his chair.

"Are you threatening me?"

"No!" Ed said. "No, I ain't threatening you."

"Then what are you talkin' about?"

"I mean, I got him," Ed said. "I got him tied up, and I got his gun. He's gotta be worth somethin', right?"

"Are you tellin' me you took Clint Adams, relieved him of his gun and tied him up?"

"That's right."

"Why?"

"We was gonna get a ransom for him."

"Ah," Ken said, "you kidnapped him."

"Right."

"And what went wrong?"

Ed shrugged and said, "We don't know who to get a ransom from."

Ken sat back and laughed.

"So you want us to ransom him?"

"No," Ed said, "I want you to buy him."

"Buy him?"

"And do what you want with him."

Ken sat back in his chair and regarded the young man.

"Prove it."

"What?"

"Prove to me that you've got him."

"How do I do that?"

"Bring me his gun."

"I can do that," Ed said.

"Then do it," Ken said. "You bring me the Gunsmith's gun, and I'll buy him from you."

"For how much?"

"We'll wipe out your debt."

Ed shook his head.

"We need more than that."

"Well," Ken said, "bring me the proof, and then we'll talk."

Ed stood up, his cup of coffee untouched.

"I'll bring it to you," he promised.

"You know, kid," Ken said, "I like you. You remind me of me."

Ed didn't know what to say to that. He didn't even know if he liked it.

"Go on," Ken said, before he could think of a reply. "Get goin', and don't keep me waitin' to long."

"I won't," Ed said. "I'll be back soon."

As Ed went out the batwings Ken said, "Big Bill, bring me a whiskey!"

THIRTY

As Ed came out of the saloon, down the street Julia was in front of the boutique and spotted him. She waited until he was within earshot and called, "Ed! Eddie!"

He turned at the sound of her voice, then looked unhappy when he saw her. He seemed to consider ignoring her, then put his head down and walked over.

"What are you doing here?" she demanded. "You're supposed to be looking after Sam."

"He's fine," Ed said. "Nathan's with him."

"Why were you in the saloon?"

"Don't worry, Julia," Ed said. "I've got everything under control."

"Ed—"

"I have to go," he said. "I'll see you at home."

"Ed—" she said, but he turned and ran off. She looked down the street at the Purple Garter. The only reason he could have been there was to see the Colter Brothers. She was afraid that her brother was taking on more than he would be able to handle—alone.

She went back inside and hoped Gloria would not fire her for having to leave.

*****

Clint heard footsteps again, too soon for somebody to be bringing him food.

"Clint?"

"Julia?"

"I think I have a way to get in," she said.

"Okay," he said. "Go ahead."

Suddenly, there was a bang, then another. The entire shack shook, and then something broke through one wall. He saw the head of a sledge hammer come through, get stuck, pull out, and then come through again. One more hit and there was a space large enough for somebody to fit through.

Julia came through and looked at him. She was breathing hard and sweating, and suddenly the smell was like pure sex to him. She was too beautiful, especially in that setting. His body reacted, even though he was trussed up.

"I don't know what to do," she said.

"Well, you can start by untying me."

"No."

"Then what?"

"I—I need to do something first, because I may not get another chance."

He got down on her knees in front of him and began to undo his trousers…

*****

Julia was surprised. When she walked through the opening she'd made in the wall of the shed and looked down at Clint Adams she felt something she'd never felt before. They were in close quarters, he'd been in there for a long time, she was sweating, and yet the comingling of their scents made her so excited she had only one thought…

*****

This close to her, as she leaned over him and pulled his trousers down, the smell of her was overpowering. By the time she had his shorts down he had a full, raging erection. She took a moment to sit back and look at it, her eyes wide, and then she reached out and touched it, stroked it, and Clint felt his eyes almost roll up into his head. This was the last thing he expected, and yet it seemed so right. The fact that he was tied hand and foot just seemed to intensify the experience.

She looked up at him while holding him in both hands and leaned into kiss him. It was tentative at first, because she wasn't very experienced with kissing, obviously. But as the kiss deepened she melted into it, became emotional, even started to cry. After that she couldn't pull her skirt up and her bloomers down fast enough. She straddled him, reached down to hold him and then sat down on him, taking the length of him into her slowly until she was sitting firmly on him, and he filled her completely.

"Oh, God..." she moaned, tears rolling down her eyes.

He couldn't grab hold of her, so all he could do was move with her as she began to ride him up and down, gasping every time she sat back down on him and he lifted his hips to meet her. She was wet, so wet and slick and hot, her steamy slime covering his thighs.

She leaned forward so he could kiss her warm neck. She peeled down the top of her dress so he could see her pert, round breasts with their hard pink nipples. Leaned forward so he could take them in his mouth. She moaned as he bit and sucked on her nipples.

Finally, he couldn't take it anymore.

"My hands," he said. "Untie me. I want to hold you."

She leaned against him, reached behind him, and undid his bonds. His hands were numb from being tied so long, and he fumbled a bit at first, but eventually he held her breasts in his hands, enjoying their weight, their warmth, lifted them to his mouth again so he could enjoy their taste.

She continued to ride him the whole time and when waves of pleasure began to overtake her she almost panicked, but he held her, soothed her, explained to her that she was having an orgasm for the first time. Then, as she continued to bounce up and down on him, he roared and exploded into her. .

THIRTY-ONE

fter she untied his feet Clint pulled his trousers back up and tried to stand. Julia pulled her dress back up, stood, and allowed him to lean on her. Together, they went out of the shed through the opening she'd made, but as they did they brushed against the side, causing the wall to fall in. When they were outside the entire shed collapsed, the roof falling in and the walls falling down.

The debris kicked up dust as they backed away from it, Clint leaning heavily on Julia. They stood there a few moments until he could stand on his own.

"Why did you let me out?" he asked.

"My brothers are in trouble," she said. "I think the Colters might kill them."

"Nathan, too?"

"I don't know," she said, "but I'm afraid." She turned to face him. "Please don't take revenge on them for what they did. They were...foolish boys."

"Foolish boys who almost caved in my skull," he said, putting his hand to the back of his head.

"Ed was in town, at the Purple Garter. I think he went to see the Colters."

"To do what?"

"I'm afraid...I'm afraid he wants to sell you to them."

"And what would they do to me if they bought me from your brother?" he asked.

She hesitated, then said, "Kill you, I think."

"And you don't want me to take my revenge against your brothers?"

"Sam is home in bed. He was beaten up. Nathan is only twelve. He did what his older brother told him. And Ed...Ed is headstrong. If you want to take revenge, then take it on me. They're all my responsibility. They have been since my parents died."

Clint rubbed his hands together and stamped his feet, trying to get the blood flowing again.

"Well," he said, "I'm certainly not going to take revenge against you, Julia." He looked her in the eye. "Not after today."

She blushed and looked away.

"The Colters will want proof from Ed that he has me," Clint said.

"You think they'll come here?"

"No," he said, "he won't tell them where I am. He's not that stupid, is he?"

"No," she said, "he's not stupid. Just foolish."

"So," Clint said, "he'll have to show them something of mine."

"But...what?"

He touched his hip and said, "My gun. Ed took it from me. He must have hid it somewhere."

"In our house," she said.

"Can we get there before he does?"

"No," she said, "no, we took...too much time."

"So no doubt he'll go to the Purple Garter and give the Colters my gun. He may have done it already."

"So what do we do?"

"Well," Clint said, "I'll need another gun. Do you have one at the house?"

"Just a rabbit rifle."

"Then I'll have to get one," he said. "You know, when he tries to give me to the Colters and sees I'm not here he'll have to explain it to them. He'll be in trouble."

She looked at the collapsed shack.

"He'll probably think I somehow got out myself."

"They'll come looking for you, won't they?"

"Probably," he said. "But I'll be looking for them, too, since I'll be wanting my gun back. And then there's my horse. If they touch my horse I'll have to kill them." He looked at her. "How many of them are there?"

"There are three brothers, but more gang members."

"All right," he said. "I think first I need to get cleaned up, maybe have some food. Aren't you supposed to be at work?"

"I am," she said. "I told Gloria I had something to do."

"Well," he said, "you go back to work."

"What are you going to do?"

"I'm going to go to your house and make sure Sam and Nathan are safe," he said.

"You can wash up there, and eat."

"All right," he said, "and then I'll have to go and find a gun. And maybe I can find Ed before he gets himself into too much trouble."

"All right."

"How much do your brothers owe the Colters?"

"I don't know," she said. "Sam said only Ed knows. But they lost money playing poker."

"Mmm," he said. "All right. Tell me how to get to your house."

"Can you make it?" she asked. "Do you need me to help you walk?"

"No," he said, "I think I can walk. My legs are kind of weak, but that's not from being tied up."

She blushed again.

THIRTY-TWO

lint followed Julia's directions to the house she shared with her brothers. When he got there he decided to knock, just in case somebody inside decided to take a shot at him with their rabbit rifle.

The door was opened by Nathan.

"Clint!" the boy said. "Did Ed let you out? I told him he should let you out."

"No," Clint said, "Ed didn't let me out, Julia did. Can I come in?"

"Sure."

Clint entered and closed the door behind them. The house looked barely big enough for the four siblings to share.

"Where's Sam?" he asked.

"Still in bed," Nathan said. "He's got broke ribs and some bruises. Should I get him?"

"No, no," Clint said, "let him rest."

"Wait a minute," Nathan said, frowning. "Does Ed know Julia was gonna let you out?"

"No, he doesn't."

"He's gonna be mad."

"Probably, but he was going to sell me to the Colter Brothers, Nathan."

"He said maybe he would do that."

"And do you know what the Colters would do with me if he did?"

"No."

"They'd kill me."

Nathan's eyes widened. "We gotta tell Ed!"

"That's what I intend to do," Clint said, "but first I need to clean up. I've been in that shed a long time."

"Okay," Nathan said. "Do you wanna take a bath?"

"I do," Clint said, "but I don't have time. I'll just wash. And maybe you could get me one of Ed's shirts?"

"He's only got two," Nathan said, "and one's dirty. He's wearin' the other one."

"Okay, then I'll have to make this one work."

"Wait," Nathan said. "We still got some of Pa's shirts."

"Your father?" Clint asked. "Oh, I don't want to make you do that."

"Naw, it's okay," Nathan said. "I can get you one. You go ahead and wash up."

"Okay, Nathan," Clint said. "Thanks."

*****

Ed entered the Purple Garter and stopped just inside the doors. There were more people there now, but Ken Colter was still seated at the same table. Neither of his brothers was with him, yet, which suited Ed just fine. He walked to the table with Clint Adams' gun belt over his shoulder.

"There you are," Ken Colter said. "Is that it?"

"This is it."

"Put it on the table."

Ed hesitated.

"How am I supposed to examine it if you don't put it down?" Ken asked.

Ed hesitated again, then took it off his shoulder and put it down.

Ken reached for the gun and slid it from its holster.

"Doesn't look like much," he said. "How do I know it's really his?"

"I took it off him," Ed said, "while he was unconscious."

"So you say," Ken said. He put it back in its holster. "I'm not convinced. I thought his gun would look more... special. You know, expensive. This is simple."

"But...it's his."

"I think you need to show me more."

"Like what?"

"You need to show me him."

THIRTY-THREE

"I swear," Ed said, "he was in there."

They were staring at the collapsed tool shed. Ed had led Ken out there, agreeing to prove he had Clint by showing him to the man.

Ken moved in among the debris, moved some wood around, kicked some away, then came back and stood in front of Ed.

"Well, he's not there now."

Ed hurried into the debris, began searching, came up with some rope and returned to Ken, clutching it in his hand.

"These are the ropes I tied him with."

Ken took them, examined them.

"They're not cut," he said. "Somebody untied him." He looked at Ed. "Who would do that?"

"Nobody."

"Your little brother, maybe?"

"No!" Ed said. "He's at home with Sam."

"What about your pretty little sister?"

"She doesn't know where we were holdin' him."

Ken went to the debris again, found the door, and stood it up. The padlock was still on it. Then he moved some of the fallen walls around until he found the one with the hole in it.

"Somebody pounded a hole in this wall." He looked around again, found the sledgehammer. "Recognize this?"

"It's a sledgehammer," Ed said. "It could've come from anywhere." But it didn't. He knew the hammer had come from his house.

Ken discarded the hammer and the ropes.

"Okay," he said, "you had him."

"We still have his gun," Ed said. It was over his shoulder again.

Ken reached out and removed the gun belt from his shoulder.

"So we do," Ken said, "and he's gonna come for it."

"He's gonna kill me, first," Ed said, "now that he's free. I need some money."

"I tell you what I'll do," Ken said. "For the gun I'll forgive the debt you and your brother owe us."

"B-but, I need more than that."

Ken poked Ed in the chest with his index finger and said, "Take what you can get, boy."

Ken turned and walked away from Ed, then stopped and turned around.

"And take my advice," Ken said. "Don't play poker, anymore."

He walked away, leaving the boy with his shoulders slumped miserably.

*****

Greg Colter had the redhead on her hands and knees in bed and was ramming his cock into her from behind when the door to the room slammed open.

"Get dressed!" Ken barked. "We got business."

"What the hell-" Greg complained.

"You want the Gunsmith or not?"

Greg quickly pulled out of the girl, got to his feet, and faced his brother. His cock, still glistening with the girl's juices, prodded the air. Ken ignored it.

"I want the Gunsmith," Greg said.

"Get dressed," Ken said. "I gotta get Jerry. Meet us downstairs."

Ken left. Greg stepped forward and slammed the door, turned to the girl. She had turned over and was sitting with her arms wrapped around her knees.

"We done?" she asked, Greg completely missing the hopeful tone in her voice.

"He has to go to the hotel to get my brother," Greg said. "We have time. Turn around."

*****

By the time Greg finished with the girl and got down to the saloon, Ken and Jerry were sitting there with beers. Greg went to the bar, got one for himself, and joined his brothers.

"God," Jerry said, waving at the air, "you smell like a cheap whore."

"Only kind you can get in this town," Greg said. He sipped his beer, looked at the gun belt and gun in the center of the table. "What's this?"

"This," Ken said, putting his hand on it, "is the Gunsmith's gun."

"You're kiddin'." He put the beer down, reached for the gun, and slid it from the holster.

"It looks ordinary," Jerry said.

"That's what I said," Ken agreed.

Greg hefted the gun and said, "That's because neither of you knows about guns. This gun is weighted perfectly."

"If you say so," Ken said. "Give it here." He took it and slid it back into the holster.

"How'd you get it?" Greg asked.

Ken explained the chain of events to his brothers, who couldn't believe it.

"Those kids?" Jerry asked.

"I told you," Ken said, "the older one, Ed, reminds me of me."

"So whatta we do now?" Greg asked.

"We have his gun," Ken said, "that means the Gun-smith is gonna come lookin' for us, eventually. All we have to do is wait, and you'll get your chance, Greg."

They lifted their beers and toasted to Greg's chance.

THIRTY-FOUR

After Clint got cleaned up and put on the fresh shirt Nathan had given him, he ate some cold chicken, then checked on Sam, who's eyes widened when Clint entered his room. He shrank back in the bed.

"Take it easy," Clint said. "I'm not going to hurt you."

"H-how'd you get out?"

"Julia was smart enough to let me out," Clint said, "so I can save you idiots from the Colter Brothers."

"W-where's Ed?"

"I think he went to town to talk to the Colters," Clint said.

"They'll kill 'im!"

"I'm not going to let that happen," Clint said. "Sam, did Ed have a gun around here, other than that rifle you use to shoot squirrels and rabbits?"

"H-he had a pistol."

"Where is it?"

Sam pointed to one of the other beds. Clint found the gun wrapped in a cloth under the bed. He unwrapped it, looked at it, then dropped it on the bed.

"That would blow up in the hand of anyone who tried to fire it," he said. "I'm going to have to get a gun somewhere else."

"You gonna buy one?" Nathan asked from the door.

"My guess is your brother already sold my gun to the Colters," Clint said. "That means they know I don't have one. If I go into town unarmed, I'm dead." He looked at Nathan. "Nathan, you're gonna have to do me a favor."

"Sure, Clint," Nathan said, "anything."

Clint looked at Sam and said, "You stay in bed."

"I'm hungry."

"I'll get you something," Clint said, "as soon as I send Nathan on his errand."

Clint and Nathan left the room and went to the kitchen table.

"I need you to go to my room," Clint said. "I have another gun in my saddlebag."

"Okay," Nathan said, "I'll get it and bring it back."

"It's smaller," Clint said, referring to the Colt New Line he often used as a hideaway gun. "You'll be able to put it in your belt and hide it under your shirt."

"All right."

"Make sure you do that," Clint said. "I don't want anyone to see you walking the street carrying a gun. Understand?"

"I understand."

"I don't have a key to give you," Clint said. "You'll have to figure something out."

"No problem."

"All right," Clint said. "Go, fast as you can."

"Yessir!" Nathan said, eager to make up for what his brothers had done to Clint.

As he went out the door Clint grabbed a couple of cold chicken legs and took them in to Sam.

*****

Ed didn't know what to do or where to go. Things had not turned out the way he wanted them to. He found himself wandering over to the livery, to the area behind it where they had hit Clint over the head. He sat down on the edge of a horse trough and hung his head. Then he raised his head and looked at the back of the livery.

What if he could sell the Colters Clint Adams' horse?

*****

Julia went back to work, apologizing again to Gloria for having left. She put her head down, determined to work hard the rest of the day, but she was still thinking about her brothers and Clint Adams. Mostly, she was worried about Nathan. She hoped that Clint would be able to help her brothers get out from under their debt, without anything happening to Nathan.

*****

Nathan ran all the way to Clint's hotel and went around to the back. He had snuck into the hotel before, and knew there was a window back there he could always open from outside.

He snuck in and went up the stairs to the second floor. Clint had told him the room number. Even Ed didn't know that from time to time Nathan snuck into hotel rooms to see what he could pick up. If Julia ever found out she'd be furious with him.

He had a small folding knife he kept in his pocket, and he used it to slip the lock on the door and get inside. He'd learned how to do it without even leaving any marks on the door. He didn't think even Ed knew how to do that.

Inside the room he found Clint's saddlebags and reached inside for the gun. When he found the .32 caliber Colt New Line he wasn't disappointed. Clint had warned him it would be smaller than his other gun. He stuck it in his belt and found that it sat there comfortably. As Clint had told him, he pulled his shirt down over it.

Before leaving he looked through the saddlebags thoroughly. He found some letters and a book by Mark Twain, but nothing else that interested him. He left the room, retraced his steps, went out the window, and ran all the way back home.

THIRTY-FIVE

Clint managed to make his way to the livery stable without being seen. When he got there he saw Ed entering by the back door. He was getting there just in time to save the boy from losing some fingers.

He hurried to the back of the stall, opened the door, and entered himself.

"Sorry, son," he heard Hoss saying, "I can't let you do it."

"I tol' you, Hoss," Ed said. "Clint Adams sent me to get the horse."

"I ain't givin' that animal to anybody but him," Hoss said.

Clint stepped into the open. The two men were facing each other in front of Eclipse's stall.

"Let him try, Hoss."

Both turned and looked at him.

"What?"

"Let him try to take the horse," Clint said. "Let's see what happens."

"Mr. Adams," Hoss said, "your horse won't go with him. It'll either take a piece out of him or kick him to death."

"Maybe," Clint said, "but let's see." He looked at Ed. "Go ahead, boy. Take him."

"H-how did you get out?" Ed asked. "I saw the shed. It was destroyed."

"I guess we got a little carried away in getting me out," Clint admitted.

"You and...who?"

"That's not for me to tell," Clint said.

"Was it Julia?"

"What's the matter, Ed," Clint said, "don't you want the horse? To sell to the Colters? My gun wasn't enough?"

"T-they didn't give me any money," Ed said. "They only wiped out the poker debt."

"Isn't that good?" Clint asked.

"Yeah, but—"

"You wanted more."

"We need more," Ed said. "My family, we need it."

"So you're doing this for your family."

"Well, yeah."

Clint turned to Hoss.

"I need a gun," he said. "Do you have one?"

"You don't have one?" Hoss asked, puzzled.

"The young man here sold my gun to someone," Clint said. "I have this," he took out the Colt New Line, "which Nathan brought to me."

"And your rifle?" Hoss asked.

"It's in my room,' Clint said. "I couldn't have Nathan running through the streets with it."

"Do you want me to go and get it?" Ed asked.

Clint looked at him.

"I thought you were here to steal my horse."

"I—I couldn't think of what else to do," he said. "I'm sorry."

"Well, I could use the rifle," Clint said, "but what I really need is a good pistol."

"I got a pistol at home," Ed said.

"Yes, I saw it," Clint said. "It's a good thing you never tried to fire it. It would have blown up in your hand."

"I got a shotgun," Hoss said. "Over-and-under Greener."

"A shotgun could work," Clint admitted. "How old is it?"

Hoss hesitated, then said, "Eighteen fifty-nine, or so."

"Clean?"

"I keep it clean."

"Let me have a look at it."

"I'll get it."

"And I can go and get the rifle," Ed said.

"I don't have a key," Clint said, "and I don't want anyone to see you."

"Who do you think showed Nathan how to get into a locked room?" Ed asked. "I'll be right back."

The boy left, and Clint was alone with Eclipse.

"Well, we've done it again, boy," Clint said, stroking the Darley Arabian's flank. "Gotten ourselves in the middle of somebody else's mess."

The horse turned his head to look at Clint.

"Oh yeah, I know," Clint said, "I didn't do it myself. After all, they did kidnap me and lock me up. By all rights I should saddle up and we should ride out—except that I want my gun back."

Hoss returned at that moment with his Greener and a handful of shells.

Clint took the shotgun, broke it open, examined it. The hostler did, indeed, keep it clean, but it was an old gun.

"Let's go out back, Clint said. "I'd like to fire it."

"Sure, of course," Hoss said.

They went out the back door and Clint loaded two shells into the shotgun.

"The corral needs repairin'," Hoss said. "Fire at one of the posts."

"Okay." Clint turned to the corral, fired one barrel, and then the other. The shot chewed up the wood of the post nicely, but...

"It seems to shoot low," Clint said. "I can compensate for that." He turned to Hoss. "Do you have a gunsmith shop in town?"

"We did," Hoss said. "He left town when the new mayor took office. Didn't like the way things were changin'."

"I see."

"Do you wanna use the shotgun?"

"I can make it work."

Hoss handed him the rest of the shells, which Clint put in his pockets.

"Send Ed out here when he gets back, will you?" Clint asked.

"Sure."

Clint sat on a barrel, holding the shotgun, and waited for Ed.

THIRTY-SIX

Ed came through the back door, carrying Clint's rifle. He carried it over to where he was sitting, but didn't hand it over right away.

"Ed?" Clint said. "The rifle?"

"You ain't gonna shoot me with it, are you?"

"Why would I do that?"

"Because I kidnapped you."

"Ed," Clint said, "if I wanted to shoot you, I could have done it with this shotgun."

Ed looked at the shotgun in Clint's hand, then said, "Oh, right," and handed over the rifle.

"Okay," Clint said, "thanks." He put it on the ground leaning against the barrel. "Ed, can you tell me how many members of the gang there are?"

"Including the brothers?"

"Yes, including the brothers."

Ed thought a moment, then said, "There are seven."

"I see."

"You're not plannin' on facin' all seven, are you?"

"Well," Clint said, "I guess that'll be up to them, won't it?"

"Well, you should know that Greg fancies himself a fast gun," Ed said.

"I'd heard that."

"So he'll want to try you himself, first."

"But he has brothers," Clint said, "and they'll be there. So will the gang. You can get that if I kill him, they'll act immediately."

"Even if you kill him in a fair fight?"

"When you're dealing with a gang like this, Ed," Clint said, "there's no such thing as a fair fight."

"That don't seem right."

"What would you do to keep your brothers safe? Or your sister?"

"Well...anythin', I guess."

"And what would you do if somebody killed one of them?"

Ed thought a moment, then said, "I think I see your point."

"I thought you might."

"But...I can't let you do that," Ed said. "Not alone. After all, you're doin' this to keep the Colters from kil- lin' us."

"Well," Clint said, "that's one reason. The other one is they have my gun."

"Still," Ed said, "I should back your play."

"And Sam and Nathan?" Clint asked. "Do you want them to back our play?"

"No, sir," Ed said. "They're just kids. They'll get themselves killed."

"Tell me something, Ed," Clint said.

"What?"

"Have you ever killed a man?"

"No, sir."

"Have you ever even fired a gun at a man?" Clint asked further.

"No, sir," he said, "but if you give me the shotgun, I'm sure I can—"

"My point is," Clint said, "it's a big thing to fire a gun at a man. If you've never done it, I can't have you backing any play I make."

"Why not?"

"If it comes right down to it," Clint said, "and you can't do it. or if you freeze, even for a second, you could get me killed."

"But—"

"Or get yourself killed," Clint went on, cutting him off. "How would I explain that to Julia?"

Ed thought a moment, then asked, "B-but what about the law?"

"The sheriff won't do anything," Clint said. "It's not his job. No law's been broken."

"But if they kill you—"

"Then he'll have to decide if he wants to do something," Clint said, "but not before."

"Then...how will you do it? How will you face seven men?"

"I need a pistol," Clint said, "and a holster. Preferably my pistol and holster."

"What if I can get it for you?"

"How?"

"I can steal it."

"Do you know where it is?"

"The last time I saw it, they had it on a table in front of them in the Purple Garter."

"How would you steal it?"

"I don't know," Ed said. "I'd have to figure that out."

"Well, Ed," Clint said, "can I assume you've stolen things before?"

"Oh, yes, sir," Ed said, "that's somethin' I have done before...uh, I'm ashamed to say, of course."

Clint nodded, smiled, and said, "Of course."

THIRTY-SEVEN

lint decided that he and Ed should figure out how to steal the gun back together.

"There must be someplace we can talk where we won't be seen," Clint said. "I don't want word getting around about where I am."

"I can only think of one place," Ed said, "but that's only if Julia's boss doesn't mind."

"The boutique?"

"No," Ed said, looking puzzled, "the dress shop."

"Right, right," Clint said. "Okay, can you get us there without us having to walk down Main Street?"

Ed grinned and said, "Just follow me."

*****

When they got to the back door of the shop, Clint waited while Ed went around to the front. Eventually, Clint heard the door unlock and then Gloria Knight appeared, a bemused look on her face.

"I understand you want to use my shop as a sort of safe haven."

"With your permission, of course."

"Come inside," she said, stepping back.

He entered and closed the door, turned to find himself in a combination storeroom/office.

"Have you gotten yourself into trouble?" she asked, folding her arms.

"I suppose I have."

"Through no fault of your own?"

"Naturally."

"I suppose that comes with being who you are."

"Unfortunately."

"All right, then," she said. "I'll send your coconspirator back. Do you mind if I keep Julia working?"

"I'd prefer it," Clint said. "I don't really want her to hear what's going on."

"Why?" Gloria asked. "What is going on?"

"I'm just trying to get Julia's brothers out of trouble," he explained.

"I'll send him back."

She went through the doorway, and several minutes later Ed appeared.

"So," he asked, "what do we do?"

Clint laid his rifle and the shotgun aside and sat down on a crate.

"We need to figure out a way to steal my gun back," Clint said.

"Why don't you leave that to me, Mr. Adams?" Ed asked. "I got you into this mess. And I probably have more experience stealing than you do."

"Tell me," Clint asked, "how would you do it?"

"Well...I could just walk in and snatch it," Ed said. "Before they realized what I did I'd be out the batwings and into the street."

"Unless they shot you before you could get to the door," Clint pointed out.

"I'm a fast runner."

"And Greg is a fast gun, right?"

"He thinks he is."

"Has he ever demonstrated this speed with a gun?" Clint asked.

"You mean has he killed anybody?" Ed asked. "Yeah, he has, but that don't mean he's so fast."

"If he's faced men with a gun and come out on top, then he's got some talent with a gun," Clint said. "It doesn't even have to be speed. You see, the fastest gun doesn't always win."

"Really?" Ed seemed puzzled.

"Usually it's the man with the steadier hand."

Ed looked down at his hand, which showed a slight tremor.

"You're nervous now," Clint said, "just at the thought of walking into that saloon."

"I was nervous when I walked in before, with your gun," Ed confessed. "That didn't stop me."

"That's good," Clint said. "But I can't put you right in the middle of the action, Ed. You'd end up getting killed."

"Well," Ed said, "you can't go in there alone and get your gun."

Clint thought a moment, then asked, "How much do you know about the bartender, Big Bill?"

"He owns the Purple Garter," Ed said. "People in town say he'd do anything to keep it the way it is."

"And that's where the Colters do their drinking," Clint said. "Is he friends with them?"

"I don't think so."

"No, I don't, either," Clint said. "Not from what I saw the few times I was there. But I need to know for sure. I need to talk to...Ed, why don't you go out and stay with your sister, and ask Mrs. Knight to come back here for a moment."

"Yeah, okay."

Ed went to the front, and moments later Gloria Knight reappeared.

"Ed said you need me?"

"I'm sorry to interrupt your work."

"That's all right," she said. "It was a slow day, so I put out the closed sign."

"Ah, well..."

"Don't worry about it," Gloria said. "What can I do for you?"

"Well, I need to talk to a business owner," he said.

"And here I am!" she said, striking a pose.

"Yes," he said. "How well do you know the other business owners in town?"

"That depends on who you mean?"

"The owner of the Purple Garter, Big Bill..."

"Benson," she supplied.

"Really?"

She nodded.

"Okay," he said "Big Bill Benson...what I know about him I got from him. He's not a big supporter of the new mayor."

"Not at all."

"Do you know much about him beyond that?"

She shrugged. "Ask me a specific question."

"How close is he to the Colter Brother Gang?"

"Big Bill? He's just a saloon owner. The gang likes to drink there, and he needs all the business he can get, so he puts up with them."

"I see. That's good."

"Why?"

"Well," he said, "I may need his help to get in there and get my gun back."

"How did they get your gun?"

"It's a long story," Clint said, "but if I'm going to face the gang to get Julia's brothers out of trouble, I'll need my gun."

"The whole gang?" she asked. "By yourself?"

"Looks like it."

"How many is that?"

"According to Ed, seven."

"Seven against one?" she asked. "Are those odds that you prefer?"

"No," he said, "but with my gun, it doesn't seem so bad."

"Does it have to be your gun?"

"Well...I prefer my own gun, but a good gun would do the trick, I suppose. Ed had one, but it was old and wouldn't have fired."

"Wait."

She went to a corner of the room, where she removed a few bolts of cloth from the top of a chest, then opened it and took something out. She walked over to him with something wrapped in a muslin cloth.

"Here," she said. "Will this do?"

She held it out and he unfolded the cloth to reveal a holster and pistol. The holster had been well oiled. He slid the gun out, found himself holding a .44 Remington that had been well cared for. It was the 1875 model that fired centerfire cartridges.

"Where did you get this?"

"Everybody thinks I'm just this woman who runs a dress shop, but I've done things in my life," she said, "and I've known people. Years ago I knew man who owned this gun, and when he died he left it to me."

"And you've kept it all this time?"

"Kept it, and took care of it," she said. "I don't know why, but maybe this is why. Maybe it was so you could use it."

Clint hefted the gun, checked the action and the barrel. It passed all his tests. All that remained was to fire it, but...

"Yes," he said, "yes, this just might do..."

THIRTY-EIGHT

lint took the gun out back and fired a few test shots, then came back in. He strapped on the holster, put the gun in, then drew it out a few times. By the time he was done both Julia and Ed had joined them in the back room.

"Where did that come from?" Ed asked.

"Just something Mrs. Knight had lying around," Clint said.

The brother and sister turned to look at the woman curiously. Gloria just shrugged.

"So now you have a gun," Julia said. "You don't have to go and get yours back."

"No," Clint said, "this just means I'll be using this gun to get my gun back."

"But why?" Julia asked. "A gun is a gun."

"Don't listen to her, Clint," Ed said. "She's just a silly girl."

Julia slapped her brother on the shoulder.

"It's a matter of principle, Julia," Clint explained. "I want what's mine. It would be the same if they had taken my horse."

"So what now?" Gloria asked. "You march into the Purple Garter, guns blazing?"

"No," Clint said, "I think I'm going to go and talk to the sheriff."

"I thought you said the Sheriff couldn't do anything," Ed said.

"I still think I should let him know what's going on," Clint said. "After all, it's his town. And maybe he'll have a suggestion."

"You really think so?" Gloria asked. "The sheriff doesn't strike me as being very smart."

"No, I get the same feeling," Clint said, "but he is the law, and after it's all over, I don't relish him trying to toss me into jail."

"You wouldn't let him do that, would you?" Ed asked.

"No, I probably wouldn't," Clint said, "but I don't relish that, either."

"What should I do?" Ed asked.

"Go back home and watch over Nathan and Sam."

"But—"

"Ed, I need to know that you're safe. I need to do this with a clear head." He looked at Julia. "And you stay here." He looked at Gloria. "Both of you."

"You're just going to walk up the street to the sheriff's office?" Julia asked.

"Now that I have this," Clint said, slapping the gun on his hip, "yes, that's exactly what I'm going to do."

THIRTY-NINE

Jerry Colter was standing at the bar in the Purple Garter waiting for three beers when he looked out the front window. He squinted, moved closer to the window to get a better look, then turned and rushed to the table his brothers were seated at.

"I just saw him."

"Saw who?" Ken asked.

"Adams," Jerry said, "the Gunsmith."

"Where?" Greg asked, looking around.

"Just outside," Jerry said. "He was walkin' by."

"Goin' where?" Ken asked.

"I don't know—"

"Well, go and find out before it's too damn late!" Ken snapped at him.

"Right!" Jerry turned and ran out the batwings.

"I should go," Greg said, standing up. "Might as well take him in the street—"

"No," Ken said, "not yet, but while you're up, go and get the drinks."

"Ken—"

"Go!"

Reluctantly, Greg Colter went to the bar.

*****

Clint reached the sheriff's office and entered without knocking. Sheriff Gregorius was seated behind his desk, drinking a mug of coffee.

"Mr. Adams," he said, "what can I do for you?"

"Do you mind if I sit?" Clint asked.

"Not at all," Gregorius said. "How about a cup of coffee. I just made a pot."

"That sounds good."

The sheriff got up, poured a mug of coffee, handed it to Clint, and sat back down. Clint sipped it, found it to be palatable.

"Not bad," he said.

"Now," Gregorius asked, "what can I do for you?"

"I'm afraid I'm about to have a...meeting with the Colter gang."

"A meeting?" Gregorius said. "What about?"

"Well," Clint said, "they seem to have my gun."

*****

Jerry Colter watched as Clint Adams reached the sheriff's office and went inside, then turned and ran back to the saloon. When he got to his brother's table there were three beers on it. He sat down and quickly drank down half of one.

"So?" Ken asked.

"He went to see the sheriff."

"About what?" Greg asked.

"How the hell would I know that?" Jerry asked.

"I think we can guess," Ken said. He put his hand out and laid it on Clint Adams' gun and gun belt.

"You think the sheriff's gonna come here for his gun?" Greg asked.

"Not a chance," Ken said. "He doesn't have the guts. No, Adams will talk to him, and then he'll come straight here. Greg, go and get our friend a beer."

"Our friend?"

"Get Mr. Adams a beer!"

Puzzled, Greg went to the bar.

"We gonna take him as soon as he walks in?" Jerry asked.

"Would I be buyin' him a beer if we were?"

"Then what?"

Ken looked around. The tables around them were empty. That's because nobody sat near the Colter Gang unless they had to. The rest of the gang was spread out in the room.

"We'll see."

*****

The Sheriff looked at Clint's hip.

"What's that?"

"I borrowed one," Clint said. "This one is going to help me get mine back."

"Is that so?" the lawman asked. "And how did they get your gun?"

"Let's just say they stole it," Clint said. He didn't want to tell the lawman what the Tanner boys had done. He might feel a responsibility to arrest them. He didn't know just how devoted to his job this lawman was.

"How did they—"

"The important thing here," Clint said, cutting him short, "is that they have my gun, and I want it back."

"And where do they have it?"

"The last time it was seen was on a table in the Purple Garter."

"That place," Gregorius said, shaking his head. "What do you want me to do?"

"Well," Clint said, "you might walk in there and ask them to give it back."

"I think that might be between you and them, Mr. Adams," the lawman said. "I can't see that any law's been broken yet."

"They stole my gun."

"Can you prove it?"

"They have it!"

"That doesn't mean they stole it."

Clint drank some more coffee, then put the mug down on the desk.

"Sheriff," he said, "you know what's going to happen if I have to walk in there and get my gun back."

"Well," Gregorius said, "they might give it to you."

"Or, they might try to kill me," Clint said. "I understand Greg fancies himself a fast gun."

"He actually is pretty fast," the sheriff said. "I've seen him."

"So then you'd be interested to see how he does against me."

The sheriff thought about the question and said, "Well, yeah, I guess so."

"Only you know it wouldn't be a fair fight."

"How do I know that?"

"Because you know those brothers," Clint said. "They'd never just stand there and let me gun down their little brother. They and the rest of the gang would step in."

"If that happens," the lawman said, "then I'd have to take action, wouldn't I?"

The man was taking exactly the stance Clint had told Ed he would take.

He stood up.

"Tell me something."

"What's that?"

"How many friends do the Colters have in town?"

"That's easy," Gregorius said. "None. Most folks are afraid of them."

"So if I get into an...altercation with the gang, I don't have to worry about anyone else joining in."

"I doubt it," the lawman said. "I'm pretty sure it would just be between you and them."

"Okay, then," Clint said. "Thanks a lot."

Clint headed for the door.

"So all that talk we had about staying out of trouble was for nothing?"

Clint stopped at the door and said, "I guess that remains to be seen. As you said, they might just give it back."

He left.

*****

After Clint Adams left his office the sheriff finished his coffee, wondering how this was going to turn out. Either the Colter Gang would kill Clint Adams, making Casa Grande one of the most famous—or infamous— towns in the West, or Clint Adams would kill the seven members of the Colter Gang in a gunfight, which—let's face it—would make Casa Grande one of the most infamous towns in the West, along the lines of Tombstone and Dodge City.

He decided to go to City Hall and tell the mayor his town's reputation was about to change drastically. He couldn't wait to see the look on the man's face.

FORTY

lint left the sheriff's office and walked directly to the Purple Garter. The business day was not yet done, so the saloon was only about half full. He approached the batwing doors, stopped just outside to take a look. He saw the three brothers sitting at a table. On the table was his gun and gun belt.

He went in.

*****

Ken felt every muscle in his younger brother's body go tense.

"Relax, Greg," he said. "Nothin's gonna happen... yet."

Ken looked around. He knew the other four members of the gang would not make a move until he did.

He turned his head and watched the Gunsmith approach.

"Mr. Adams," he said.

"That's right," Clint said. "I've come for my gun."

"This gun?" Ken asked.

"That's right."

"I paid good money for this gun," Ken said. "How do I know it's yours?"

"What if I just reached out and took it?" Clint asked.

"Why don't you sit down?" Ken suggested. "I bought you a beer. Let's talk about it."

Clint decided to play along. He sat and picked up the beer with his left hand. The younger brother was sitting across from him, throwing him hard looks.

"What's his problem?" Clint asked.

"Hmm? Oh, that's Greg. He seems to think he's faster than you with a gun, and he's itching to prove it."

"That would be a bad idea," Clint said.

"How so?" Ken asked.

"You'd lose a brother."

Greg tensed so much his chair moved.

Ken laughed.

Jerry just sat and waited for a signal from his older brother.

"Greg, the man sounds very confident," Ken said. "Whatta you think?"

"I think he's too confident," Greg said. "I think I should kill him...maybe even with his own gun."

Ken looked surprised.

"Now that sounds like a very interesting idea, Mr. Adams," Ken said. "What do you think of facing my brother while he wears your gun?"

Clint drank some beer, then said, "If we did this, I'd have to take my gun off his dead body."

"You're talkin' a good game for somebody who's past his prime," Greg Colter said.

"I'm going to ignore him," Clint said to Ken. "What if I just reached out right now and took my gun?"

"Well," Ken said, "me and my brothers would go for our guns, the rest of my men in here would go for theirs, you'd get caught in a crossfire, and some innocent bystanders would probably get killed." He made a face. "That wouldn't be good for anyone, would it?"

"Then what do you suggest?" Clint asked.

"I told my brother he'd get his chance at you," Ken said.

"Are you a man of your word?" Clint asked.

Ken spread his arms and said, "Ask anyone."

Clint pointed at Greg. "If he kills me, I want you to leave the Tanner family alone."

"Done."

"And if I kill him," Clint added, "same thing."

"You have my word," Ken said, carefully. "If you kill Greg, I won't touch the Tanner family."

Clint looked at Greg.

"When do you want to do this, boy?" he asked.

"No time like now," Greg said.

Ken put his hand out to keep Greg from getting up out of his chair.

"Two hours," Ken said.

"But why—" Ken started.

"I've got to calm this boy down," Ken said. "You want to face him at his best, don't you?"

"Oh, definitely," Clint said. "When I kill him, I don't want any excuses from anybody."

"Okay, then."

Clint looked at Greg.

"And you want me at my best, right?"

"That's right," Greg said, "because your best just ain't gonna be good enough."

"Then I'll take my gun," Clint said, pointing to the gun on the table.

Greg took a quick look at Ken.

"Sure," Ken said. "Take it."

Clint reached out carefully and lifted his gun belt off the table, then stood.

"Thanks for the beer," Clint said.

"You're welcome," Ken said.

"See you later," Greg said.

"Unless you change your mind," Clint said, "and I suggest that you do."

He turned and walked out.

FORTY-ONE

"Why not now?" Greg demanded, after Clint Adams had left.

"You've got to calm down," Ken said. "You go out there all worked up like you are now and he will kill you for sure."

"I'm so much younger than he is," Greg said. "I gotta be faster than him."

"You will be," Ken said, "if you stay calm."

"Why'd you give him his gun?" Jerry asked. They were the first words he had spoken since Clint Adams entered the saloon.

"Why not?" Ken asked. "What the hell are we gonna do with it? If Greg's gonna kill 'im , he's gonna kill 'im, no matter what gun he's wearin'."

Jerry just shrugged and went back to his drink.

"You don't think I can do it?" Greg demanded of Jerry.

"We're gonna see," was all Jerry would say.

"Jerry," Ken said, "bring the rest of the men over here. We gotta decide where to place them."

"I'm gonna kill the Gunsmith on my own, Ken," Greg said.

"I know that, kid," Ken said, "I'm just decidin' on what we're gonna do if it comes out the other way around, that's all." He leaned forward and slapped his younger brother on the shoulder. "If he does happen to kill you, he won't live two minutes after."

*****

Clint went back to Gloria's boutique, knocked on the locked door. Gloria answered and let him in. Ed and Julia were still there.

"You got your gun?" Ed said.

"I got it."

"Good," Julia said, "then we can forget about all of this craziness—"

"Not quite," Clint said. "I still have to face Greg Colter in the street."

"But why?' Julia demanded. "You have what you wanted."

"There's still the safety of you and your brothers," Clint said. "That's what I'm fighting for."

"I don't want you to die for us!" she exclaimed.

"Don't worry," he said. "I don't want that, either. Right now I think you and Ed should go be with Nathan and Sam. I'll let you know what happens."

"But—" Ed said.

"Ed." Clint said, "take your sister home."

*****

Once Julia and Ed were gone Clint removed the borrowed gun belt and handed it to Gloria.

"Thank you."

She took it and he strapped on his own gun.

"I guess it didn't do you much good."

"But it did," Clint said. "It allowed me to walk into the saloon with confidence. I didn't have to use it, but I could have."

"Come into the back room with me while I put it away," she said.

"I have some work to do outside," he said.

"I won't keep you long."

"All right."

He followed her into the back room. As they passed through the door she discarded the gun belt, turned abruptly so that they bumped into each other. Then she put her arms around his neck and kissed him soundly.

Taken by surprise Clint reached immediately, put his arms around Gloria, and returned the kiss with gusto.

When they broke apart they were both breathless.

"Gloria—"

"Shut up and undress me," she said. "In a little while you're going out there to face seven men, and who knows if I'll get this chance again?"

So he obediently stripped her dress and underthings off, revealing the full body of a woman beneath them. She had probably been a lovely young woman ten years ago, but now she was a woman, full blown, with a curvy body that featured full, brown tipped breasts, flared hips, and almost chunky buttocks.

He took her naked body in his arms, lifted her, and carried her to a bed made of bolts of cloth. He set her down, then removed the gun he had just strapped on, set it close by, undressed and went to her open arms and legs.

He kissed her, nuzzled her neck, bit and licked those luscious breasts, slid his hands beneath the full cheeks of her buttocks, pressed the head of his cock to her moist pussy and pushed. She was so wet by then that he dove into her easily. She gasped, brought her powerful legs up to wrap around his waist, and as he began to fuck her that way her breath came in heavy rasps, right in his ear, urging him on.

Suddenly she gasped into his ear, "On top, I want to be on top."

He lifted her, without withdrawing from her hot, steamy depths, turned them around so that he had his back on those bolts of cloth and now she was riding him for all she was worth, driving herself to her climax, reaching for it, chasing it and finally—treating Clint like a bucking bronco—catching it. And a moment later Clint reared up, turned her again, roared and exploded inside of her, causing her to beat on his butt with her bare heels...

*****

They dressed quietly afterward. Clint looked over at those bolts of cloth and saw the damp area on top, wondered what lucky woman was going to get a dress made out of that and wonder why she was always sexually excited whenever she wore it.

Clint grabbed his gun and strapped it on.

"Do you have to do this?" she asked.

"I always have to do this," he said. "I don't have much choice."

"And you've lived most of your life this way?"

"It's been a long road," he admitted.

They walked to the front of the store and looked out the window.

"The street's deserted," she said.

"Word's gotten out already." Clint said. He reached for his rifle and shotgun.

"Why do you need those?"

"I'm going up against seven men," he said. "I need to set the stage a little."

"So you're sure that after you kill the younger brother the rest will come for you?"

"Oh yes," he said. "They won't have much choice."

She put her hand on his arm.

"I hope you don't mind if I stay inside," she said. "I don't want to watch."

"I don't want you to," he said. "I'd prefer you stay inside."

She kissed him and said, "Good luck."

He gathered his weapons and went out the door.

FORTY-TWO

"This can't happen," the mayor said.

Walter Richards had been the Mayor of Casa Grande for just over a year, and for the most part—the Purple Garter aside—had gotten his own way in everything.

Now the fifty year old politician was staring at his young sheriff, who had brought him the news about Clint Adams and the Colter Gang.

"I know you've got the Colters under your thumb, Walter," the sheriff said, "but there's no way to stop this."

"What do you mean, under my thumb?"

"Come on, Mayor," Gregorius said. "You haven't gotten your own way this past year just by the force of your personality."

"It sounds like you think I've been using the Colters as my own personal bully boys," the mayor said.

"You said it, I didn't."

"You're walking on thin ice here, Sheriff," the mayor said. "I assume you want to keep your job."

"I do," Gregorius said, "and I know a little too much about you and your administration for you to fire me, so you better think twice about that."

The mayor stood up and looked out his window at Main Street, which was empty.

"Look at this," he said. "The town is dead."

"The town is hiding," Gregorius said, "staying out of the way."

"This Gunsmith is going to turn my town into Tombstone," Mayor Richards complained. "And you're telling me all we can do is watch?"

"Yes, sir," Gregorius said, "and right where you are, you've probably got the best seat."

Richards turned and glared at Gregorius.

"You can't gather enough deputies to stop this?"

"Not now," Gregorius said. "Everything is in motion, Mayor. This is gonna happen any minute."

"Good Lord..." the mayor said. "Why didn't you come to me sooner about this?"

"You mean you haven't heard anything about this from Ken Colter?"

Rather than answer, the mayor turned and stared out the window again, his round shoulders slumped. Just during the time he'd been in office he'd put on about twenty pounds, and he was overweight when he took office.

But at the moment he had no appetite whatsoever.

*****

"It's time," Ken Colter said.

Greg started to get up.

"Not for you," his brother said. "Jerry. Get the other boys into position."

"Right, Ken."

Jerry stood up, walked to a table where the other four gang members were seated.

"You boys all know your places?"

They all nodded, and one of them said, "Yup."

"Then get out there," Jerry said, "and keep your eyes on Ken. You move when he does, and not before."

"Got it."

They all got up and, as instructed by Ken earlier, went out the back way to take up their positions on either side of the street. Jerry went back to his table.

"You sure you wanna do this, Greg?" he asked.

"I'm damn sure!" Greg said. "And I don't want anybody interferin', understand?"

"We're just gonna be watchin', Greg," Ken said.

Greg took his gun out of his holster, checked it, and slid it back.

"Wait," Ken said.

"For what?" Greg asked.

"Let him stew," Ken said. "Let the Gunsmith wait for you, don't you go out and wait for him. Let him think about it for a while, facing a younger, faster gun. Let him think that this might be it, the time he runs into somebody faster."

"Oh, it is the time," Greg said. "Believe me."

"I do, kid," Ken said. "I believe you." What Ken believed was that his younger brother believed it. As for himself, he still wasn't all that sure.

"Jerry," he said to his middle brother, "let's you and me have one more beer before it starts."

"What about me?" Greg asked.

"No more for you, kid," Ken said. "You gotta have a steady eye and hand when you go out there."

"Look at that," Greg said, sticking out his hand. "Steady as a rock."

And it was, Ken was glad to see.

"You sure the sheriff ain't gonna get involved?" Greg asked.

"He won't."

"I don't wanna have to shoot no lawman."

"You won't," Ken said. "Sheriff Gregorius knows his place. All you gotta worry about is one thing—the Gunsmith."

"Naw," Greg said, "All he's got to worry about it me!"

FORTY-THREE

The stage was set.

But Clint didn't step out into the street. Not yet. He was standing across the street from the Purple Garter, knowing that Greg Colter would come out through the batwing doors. The rest of the gang—well, they'd probably go out the back and spread out on the street, or the rooftops. And the two brothers, they'd probably be watching from just inside the saloon.

But Clint didn't want anyone to see him waiting out in the middle of the street. If Greg thought he was nervous, it might boost the younger man's confidence. While Clint was pretty certain he'd outdraw the young man, he still didn't need anything improving Greg's performance.

So he leaned back against the building and waited.

*****

"Jerry," Ken said, "go take a look. See where he is."

Jerry got up and walked to the batwing doors, looked out over them. The street was empty. He checked across the street, but didn't see anybody. "Nothin'," he said, coming back to the table.

"Not across the street?" Ken asked.

"If he is, he's hidin'," Jerry said, sitting down.

"What's he tryin' to pull?" Greg asked.

"He's tryin' to make you nervous," Ken said.

"Or maybe," Greg said, "he left town. Maybe he ran."

"I don't think so," Ken said. "He doesn't strike me as the running type."

"So what do we do?" Greg asked.

"What do you do, you mean?" Ken asked. "You go out there and get it done."

"Now?"

"Yes," Ken said. "Now."

"Finally!" Greg said, bouncing out of his chair.

Jerry started to get up, but Ken stopped him with a look.

Greg headed for the batwing doors, and Ken moved over next to Jerry.

"I want you by the front window with a rifle," he said. "There's a chance he might spot the others out there, but you stay low. I think you're the one who's gonna have the killin' shot."

"Where will you be?"

"Right at the doorway," Ken said. "I'm gonna let Adams see me standin' there. It might distract him."

"Okay."

The watched their younger brother go out the door, then stood up and rushed to their positions.

*****

Julia didn't know what else to do, so she decided to cook. Ed helped Sam get out of bed and come to the table to sit. She put the food on the table, started to sit down, and then stopped.

"Where's Nathan?"

"Maybe in his room," Ed said. "I'll look."

Sam grimaced as he reached for a piece of beef. Ed came back from the room.

"Not there," he said. "I'll look outside."

Ed ran out the door, and Julia followed him.

"Nathan!" Ed yelled. He ran around the outside of the house, then rejoined Julia on the porch.

"Anything?" she asked.

"He's not here," Ed said.

"Oh my God," she said, "he went to town. Ed, he went to watch."

"All right, don't worry," Ed told her. "I'll bring him back."

As he started away she shouted, "You better both come back!"

FORTY-FOUR

Clint saw two things at the same time.

He saw Greg Colter come out of the saloon.

And he saw Nathan Tanner come walking down the street.

He wasn't sure what to do. Run down the street after Nathan? That would be making himself a target.

Instead, he remained on his side of the street, but moved down in the hopes of intercepting Nathan.

The kid started to run right down the center of the empty street, so when Clint came even with him he shouted, "Nathan! Nathan, goddamnit!"

Nathan stopped, looking momentarily confused, then saw Clint and ran over to him. Clint grabbed him and pulled him off the street.

"What the hell are you doing?"

"I wanted to watch," Nathan said. "What are you doin'? Ain't there gonna be a gunfight?"

"Yes, there is!" Clint said. "And you almost ran right into the middle of it. You're supposed to be home."

"I ain't goin' home. I wanna watch!" Nathan said, stubbornly.

"Then you watch from right here. Come over here." He pulled him over to a barrel in front of the hardware store. "You stay down behind here until it's over."

"You're gonna win, ain't ya, Clint?"

"Yes, Nathan," Clint said, "I'm going to win. Now you stay here! If you come running out I'll be worried about you and I'll get killed. You don't want that, do you?"

"No, sir."

"Then stay!"

"Yes, sir."

Clint turned and walked back along the boardwalk to where he had been standing originally. Greg Colter was in front of the saloon, and Clint could see his brother Ken standing in the doorway, looking over the batwing doors. After carefully examining the tableau he thought he had some of it figured, but knew there had to be some gang members on his side of the street—either in a window or on the roof.

But he had no choice.

It was time.

He stepped into the street.

*****

Greg Colter saw the kid in the street about the same time Clint Adams did. As Clint started running toward the kid Greg knew he could pick the Gunsmith off if he wanted to, but that was not the point of this. The point was to kill the Gunsmith in a fair fight, so he just stood there and waited.

And he was ready when Clint Adams stepped into the street.

*****

Ed Tanner came running down the street, stopped short when he saw two men standing across from each other. It was happening now! Where was Nathan?

"Psst," he said. "Psssst, Edddie!"

He turned his head, saw his little brother peeking up from behind a barrel in front of the Hardware Store.

"Nathan!" He ran over to him. "You're in big trouble."

"Clint already yelled at me," Nathan said.

"Well, we're goin' home. Julia's waitin'."

"Clint told me to stay here!" Nathan argued.

"Well I'm sayin' we're goin'—"

"Don't you wanna watch?" Nathan asked.

Ed turned, looked at the two men facing each other on the street.

"Well, yeah," he said, "I do wanna watch, but—"

"Well," Nathan said, "get down behind this barrel with me."

Ed knew he'd be in trouble with his sister when they got home, but he shrugged and crouched down next to his brother.

*****

Ken Colter watched from the saloon while Clint Adams stepped down into the street. He looked around, spotted his men exactly where he had placed them, knew he had to trust the others to be where they were, even though he couldn't see them. Everybody was in place to do their part.

But first, Greg had to do his part.

*****

Jerry peered out the window, being careful not to be seen. He had his rifle in his hands, ready to go. From where he was he could see the Gunsmith and the two men on the roof above and behind him. He couldn't see his brother, Greg, yet, but as soon as he and Adams were in the middle of the street he'd be able to see both of them.

*****

Clint thought he saw someone in the window of the saloon. He didn't need to be sure, just suspecting someone was there was enough. And he suspected he knew who it was—Jerry Colter.

He walked to the middle of the street, circling to his right, keeping the saloon and the other Colter brothers on his right.

FORTY-FIVE

reg circled to his right, realized that he had the sun to his back. Why would the Gunsmith give him that advantage? The only thing he could think was that the Gunsmith had lost it.

His confidence grew even more.

*****

Clint had the Colt New Line in his belt at the small of his back. It would work fine dealing with men on the ground, but anybody in a second floor window or on the roof would be out of range. But he could deal with that problem later. At the moment he figured he had at least the three Colter brothers to deal with on the ground. The other gang members would be spread out, probably higher up.

"Well, Adams," Greg Colter called out, "now you've got your gun. Go ahead and use it."

"Got all your help in place, Greg?" Clint asked. "Ken in the doorway, Jerry in the window. And the rest of the gang? Where are they? Windows? Rooftops?"

"This is just you and me, Adams," Greg said. "My brothers are stayin' out of it. I'm givin' you the first move. You better take it."

"Don't be a fool, kid," Clint said. "Take the first move. It's the best chance you'll have."

Greg shrugged. "If you insist."

The young man went for his gun. Clint was impressed. Greg actually did have some speed—just not enough.

Clint drew cleanly and fired once. The bullet hit Greg in the chest. His eyes went wide, his hand opened, and the gun fell to the ground. He'd actually been fast enough to clear leather.

As the young man fell over backward on the street, Clint looked over at Ken Colter.

Everything seemed to stop...

*****

It was deadly quiet on the street after the shot.

Ken watched as his brother fell to the ground, dead. He froze in that moment. If it wasn't for Jerry it was probable nobody else would have died, for Ken was thinking that Greg had done this to himself. None of the other men would move until he did, but Jerry got to his knees, poked his rifle right through the glass and...

*****

Clint heard the glass break, turned, and fired again. Not much of Jerry was visible through the window, but Clint put a bullet right through the man's left cye. Jerry went over backwards onto the saloon floor.

Now the rest was up to Ken Colter.

*****

Ken looked over as Jerry fell dead to the floor. The others in the saloon all hit the floor, upended tables to take cover behind them. Big Bill dropped to the floor behind the bar.

Ken looked out the door at Clint Adams, still standing in the street, waiting. The remaining Colter brother stepped through the doors.

"I told you, Colter," Clint said. "I told you this would happen."

"Yeah, you did," Ken said.

"It can stop now," Clint said, "end here. Nobody else has to die."

"Oh yeah," Ken said, "somebody else does."

Instead of going for his gun he lifted his arm, and dropped it.

Clint started running as lead began to kick up dust in the street...

*****

"Hey!" Nathan yelled. "That ain't fair!"

"Get back down," Ed yelled, yanking his brother down. "Just stay down. Clint will handle it."

They settled down to watch, and hope.

*****

Ken Colter drew his gun as his men began to fire, two from the ground, two from rooftops. He'd placed one man on each side of the street, down low and up high. Now he and they kept firing at Clint Adams, who was scrambling for cover behind a horse trough.

Ken waved at the two men who were on the ground to join him.

*****

Clint fired, giving himself as much cover as he could, until his pistol was empty. He could have employed the Colt New Line, but he decided not to. Instead, he waited...

*****

The two gang members joined Ken Colter, one on either side of him. Together they started walking across the street, toward the horse trough.

*****

Clint watched as the three men started for him. As they closed he stood up, pointed his empty pistol at them, and pulled the trigger several times so they could hear that it was empty.

*****

"You know," Ken said, "my brother said you'd lost it. You actually left yourself with an empty gun. The great Gunsmith. What a mistake."

"We all make them," Clint said. "For instance, you, standing there with two of your men right next to you. Big mistake."

The three men had stopped right in the center of the street, and now Ken Colter smiled and said, "You think so?"

"I know so."

Clint dropped his empty pistol, bent, and quickly picked up the shotgun he'd hidden behind the horse trough. Mindful of the fact that it fired low, he let go with both barrels.

The three men were far enough away from him that the shot from the double barrels spread out as it traveled.

By the time it reached the three men, it tore through all of their bodies, causing the three of them to literally fly back a few feet before they hit the ground, dead.

Clint dropped the shotgun and picked up the hidden rifle. As a man on the roof across from him stood to fire, he beat him to it, firing one accurate shot with his rifle. The bullet struck the man in the chest. He stiffened, dropped his rifle off the roof, and then tumbled down after it.

And then there was one...

"I don't know where you are for sure," Clint yelled out, "but you're alone now. If I was you I'd pull out."

He stood still, listening. A rifle hit the ground, thrown from a window or a roof, and suddenly he heard running footsteps, probably from a rooftop right above him.

The footsteps faded, and were gone.

He walked to the three bodies, his rifle in one hand, the Colt New Line in the other. Checking the three men, he found them all dead.

A crowd began to form in front of the saloon as the batwing doors belched out the Purple Garter customers.

"Go back inside and have a drink," Clint yelled. "It's all over."

He went back to the horse trough and picked up his empty pistol. Quickly, he ejected the empty shells, reloaded it, and slid it in his holster, then tucked the New Line behind him. When he turned he saw Sheriff Gregorius walking up the street toward him.

The lawman stopped at the three bodies, then walked to the fallen Greg Colter and looked at him before approaching Clint.

"And Jerry?"

"Is that the third brother? He's in the saloon."

"Any of them get away?"

"One, I think," Clint said. "I pretty much let him go, though. There's been enough killing."

"Oh, I agree. The mayor's pretty upset about it."

"I figured he would be."

"He'd like you to leave town as soon as possible."

"Not until tomorrow," Clint said.

"That's actually soon enough, as far as I'm concerned," Gregorius said. "I kind of like seeing him all upset."

"My pleasure to be of help."

"You know," the lawman said, "I think you coming to this town might just lead to some change around here."

"Good change?"

"Oh, yeah."

"Then again," Clint said. "Glad I could be of help."

Clint turned, saw Ed and Nathan looking at him from down the street.

"But I would like it to be tomorrow, Mr. Adams," the Sheriff added,

"Don't think that will be a problem."

He turned and walked to the two boys.

"Come on," he said, "I'll take you fellas home."

"That was somethin', Clint!" Nathan said, as they started up the street.

"That," Clint Adams, told the boy, "was nothing to be proud of."

The End

ABOUT THE AUTHOR

As "J.R. Roberts" Bob Randisi is the creator and author of the long running western series, *The Gunsmith*. Under various other pseudonyms he has created and written the "Tracker," "Mountain Jack Pike," "Angel Eyes," "Ryder," "Talbot Roper," "The Son of Daniel Shaye," and "the Gamblers" Western series. His western short story collection, *The Cast-Iron Star and Other Western Stories*, is now available in print and as an ebook from Western Fictioneers Books.

In the mystery genre he is the author of the *Miles Jacoby*, *Nick Delvecchio*, *Gil & Claire Hunt*, *Dennis McQueen*, *Joe Keough*, and *The Rat Pack*, series. He has written more than 500 western novels and has worked in the Western, Mystery, Sci-Fi, Horror and Spy genres. He is the editor of over 30 anthologies. All told he is the author of over 650 novels. His arms are very, very tired.

He is the founder of the Private Eye Writers of America, the creator of the Shamus Award, the co-founder of Mystery Scene Magazine, the American Crime Writers League, Western Fictioneers and their Peacemaker Award.

In 2009 the Private Eye Writers of America awarded him the Life Achievement Award, and in 2013 the Readwest Foundation presented him with their President's Award for Life Achievement.

PRO SE PRODUCTIONS PRESENTS

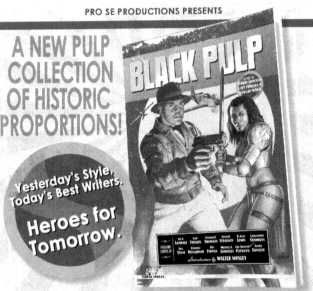

A NEW PULP
COLLECTION
OF HISTORIC
PROPORTIONS!

Yesterday's Style,
Today's Best Writers,

Heroes for
Tomorrow.

BLACK PULP is a wonderful anthology of short stories that expands the world of *Tarzan, Doc Savage, The Avenger, The Shadow, The Spider, The Phantom Detective, The Green Lama, Ki-Gor, G-8, Secret Agent X, Secret Service Operator #5,* and their contemporaries. And BLACK PULP populates this world with hitmen, boxers-turned-vigilantes, female aviators, wildmen, mercenaries-for-hire, private detectives, femme fatales, naval aviators, freedom-fighting pirates, paranormal investigators, real life lawmen, adventurers, and many more.

– Lucas Garrett, Reviewer, Pulp Fiction Reviews

Strictly adult, with a stress on a fictional world where heroes of color take center stage, readers will love these yarns of mayhem and mischief, of right hooks and upper cuts, war tales, pirates, and sleuths looking for clues among stiffs....Here, Black Pulp is gathered from the very best of the New Pulp scribes, with a genius for action and romance, drawing from the fantastic, grotesque, and magical. Read and become bewitched.

Robert Fleming, www.aalbc.com

Pulp Fiction, in many cases, is the second movement in the dialectic of inner transition. It is the antithesis of what is expected and the stepping stone to true freedom.

– Best Selling Author Walter Mosley, from his introduction to BLACK PULP

Available at amazon.com and other fine outlets.   Pro Se Productions www.prose-press.com

THE NEW ADVENTURES OF

FOSTER FADE

THE CRIME SPECTACULARIST

FEATURING CHARACTERS CREATED BY LESTER DENT

With Stories by
Adam Lance
GARCIA

Derrick
FERGUSON

Aubrey
STEPHENS

David
WHITE

H. David
BLALOCK

PRO SE PRESS

PULP OBSCURA

PULP OBSCURA IS AN IMPRINT OF PRO SE PRODUCTIONS AND IS
PUBLISHED IN CONJUNCTION WITH TITLES FROM ALTUS PRESS.

AVAILABLE AT AMAZON.COM AND WWW.PROSE-PRESS.COM

59154551R00110

Made in the USA
Lexington, KY
27 December 2016